KILL ME QUICK

QUICKSILVER: BOOK ONE

JOSIE JAFFREY

CONTENT WARNINGS & SERIES RECAPS

There is a full list of content warnings at the back of this book, and also available at Josie's website at the link on the left below.

Recaps of the Silverse books are available on Josie's website at the link on the right below.

By Josie Jaffrey

Stories from the Silverse: the World of the Silver

The Seekers Series
Killian's Dead (short story prequel, free to Josie's
subscribers)
May Day
Judgement Day
Winta's Day
Valentine's Day
Dark Days
End of Days

The QuickSilver Trilogy
Kill Me Quick
A Quick Study
Quick and the Dead
QuickSilver Omnibus Edition

The Solis Invicti Series
A Bargain in Silver
The Price of Silver
Bound in Silver
The Silver Bullet

The Sovereign Trilogy
The Gilded King
The Silver Queen
The Blood Prince

Silverse Serialised Stories
Dead Box
Dead Road

Silverse Short Stories
Encounters: Silverse Short Stories

Other Fiction

The Deluge Series
The Wolf and the Water

Short Stories
Broken Wings (collection)
Ring The Bell

1

'NO,' KULIKA SAID, crossing her arms over her chest.

'Kulika—'

'Sir, with respect, you're a bastard for even asking.'

'With *respect*?'

Kulika cringed; *bastard* might have been putting it a little strongly.

Kulika Yadav owed her life to her boss. Before he'd come along, her tortured existence had been worse than death. This life that she had now in England, full of freedom and laughter and actual friends, that was the life that she owed to Killian Drake, Baron of Oxford. Yes, they were both immortal Silver – vampires, for the uninitiated – and practically indestructible, so it wasn't as though she'd been at imminent risk of death when he'd found her in that Charleston mausoleum. But she hadn't been *living* either.

In every way that mattered, he'd saved Kulika.

She never took that for granted. She'd die for him, she'd kill for him, and then she'd bury the bodies where no one would find them. In fact, if you'd asked her yesterday, she would have told you she'd do anything at all for Baron Drake, but that was only because she'd never imagined that he'd send her back to the very hell he'd pulled her out of a century ago.

'Sir, I can't,' she pled. 'You know what'll happen if I do.'

'And you know what will happen if you don't.' He said the words softly. They weren't a threat, they were a statement of fact.

Kulika knew the truth as well as he did: if they didn't find a solution to this problem, and soon, then Baron Drake was going to die. *Really* die.

'There must be another way,' Kulika said desperately.

'I can't think of one,' he said, then he sat down in his chair, rested his elbows on his desk and put his head in his hands. 'It isn't as though I haven't been thinking about it. I never *stop* thinking about it. If she doesn't come back to me…'

She was Jack Valentine, the unlikely love of Baron Drake's life. Unfortunately, she was also a chaotic mess of a person who made terrible decisions in every sphere of her life, including those that involved her personal preservation. Long story short: she'd managed to infect herself with a poison, and now she was slowly burning to death from the inside out. There had been an antidote in production, but to make it they needed the blood of one particular Silver – Dr Jahan Khalyed – and he'd recently burned to death himself, along with every remaining trace of his blood.

Basically, Jack was fucked.

There was a muffled little *tap*. It was so quiet that Kulika wouldn't have noticed it at all without her Silver hearing. She couldn't be sure, since the baron still had his head in his hands, but she thought it might have been the sound of a teardrop hitting the blotter on his desk.

If Kulika had still been the delicate waif she'd pretended to be in her youth instead of the body-building badass she'd turned herself into, she might have fainted from shock.

Baron Drake was an island. He was a model of self-containment. If he had any vulnerable feelings at all, he never expressed them, at least not in front of other people, and he absolutely, positively didn't cry. In all the centuries of their acquaintance – friendship, even, if that wasn't too presumptuous – Kulika had never known him to loose a single tear. And now, seeing him raise his face from his hands again and rearrange his hair into its former tidy state, she saw no trace of tear marks on his face.

Perhaps she had been wrong.

But there had been that tiny *tap*.

'I'm sorry,' he said, shuffling some papers around on his desk. 'You're right. I shouldn't have asked. I'll let you get back to work.'

'Doesn't Dr Ross have any other ideas?' Kulika asked.

'This *is* her idea. We've traced the bloodlines, we've done the testing, and Dr Khalyed's only possible viable descendant went missing in Charleston in December.'

'*One* living descendant?' Kulika said incredulously.

'That's right,' he confirmed. 'Just one.'

Bugger.

Kulika had been so hoping there would be another option. Dr Ross thought it was possible – not likely, but *possible* – that the blood of one of Dr Khalyed's human descendants could be substituted for his to make the antidote Jack needed to survive. That descendant would have to be turned Silver before their blood was usable, and even then the genetic similarity might not be sufficient, but it was the only hope Jack had. It was a long shot, either way, but there was at least *some* hope.

But why did the only viable candidate have to be in Charleston, of all places?

'And you're *sure* Bartholomew took her?' Kulika asked. 'If she went missing over six months ago, then—'

'No. I'm not sure of anything.' Baron Drake pulled a file from the top drawer of his desk, then pulled a photograph from the file and stared at it for a moment.

'That's her?' Kulika asked.

'It is.' He swivelled the picture so it faced her way.

The photo showed a dark-haired, red-lipped, brown-skinned woman. She looked about thirty, maybe a little younger, and she was standing in a park, squinting into the afternoon sunshine, next to a pale-skinned woman of about the same age who was only half in the photo. The half-there woman had the kind of orangey red hair that glowed in the sunlight. It reminded Kulika of countless sunsets across the water of the open Caribbean seas. The image took her back to memories she both avoided and longed for, often at the same time.

'Perhaps I can talk to Bayly,' Baron Drake said, interrupting her reverie. 'Perhaps he might recognise her.'

'Sir,' Kulika said discouragingly. 'Job Bayly won't even talk to *me* most days. He's definitely not going to talk to you.'

'Then what do you suggest?' the baron replied, desperation edging his tone into anger. He pulled himself together quickly and said, 'You're right. I'm sorry, Kulika. This isn't your problem. You just… Carry on.'

It was a dismissal.

Kulika should have taken it. Frankly, Jack had brought this on herself. She was reckless, and impulsive, and it had only been a matter of time before she'd landed herself in the shit. If it had been just Jack's life on the line, then Kulika might have been inclined to wash her hands of the whole business and walk away.

The problem was that Baron Drake was in love with Jack, and when the Silver fell in love, it had frankly terrifying consequences. The moment he fell for Jack, Baron Drake's life became bonded to hers. If she died, then through the operation of that bond, the baron would die also.

Kulika struggled to understand why any Silver would engage in romantic shenanigans at all when the stakes were that high, particularly a Silver as powerful and important as the baron. It seemed entirely too risky to be worthwhile. As the baron's head of security, Kulika avoided those kinds of entanglements on principle, so it seemed particularly unfair that she'd become embroiled in this debacle regardless. Through no fault of her own, she was now in the unenviable position of having to protect Jack, someone who tended to hurl herself headfirst into trouble, all in order to protect the baron, her sworn master. Apparently, that also required Kulika to walk voluntarily back into her own personal hell.

'Give me the photo,' she said with a sigh.

'No, Kulika,' the baron said, covering the snapshot with his hands. 'You're right. I can't ask you to—'

'Just give me the damn photo. Sir.' Kulika snatched it from under his fingers and took a picture of it on her phone before returning it to him.

'I can't ask you to do this,' he said.

'And you're not asking, sir. But if I'm not back in a week, send Hugo, will you?'

'Kulika, I… I don't know what to say. Jack and I—'

'I'm not doing this for Jack,' she said, then she turned and left the office before she could change her mind.

If it were just for Jack, Kulika would have told the baron to go swivel. Not in so many words, perhaps, but she would truly rather have let Jack die than go back to that dark-cornered, godforsaken mansion in South Carolina.

But for Baron Drake, after all he'd done for her, after all the pieces of himself he'd sacrificed to give her this life that she loved…

She couldn't just let him die.

2

PATIENCE QUICK COULD claim neither of the attributes that formed her full name. She'd never understood the point of delaying gratification, and although she was a keen runner, she rarely paced above a jog, particularly in the heavy heat of a Charleston summer. *Impatience Steady* would have suited her better. Really, she had no idea what her birth parents had been thinking.

It could have been worse, she supposed. At least she wasn't called Chastity or, god forbid, Temperance. Neither would have served her well in her current situation.

'Get you another?' the bartender offered.

'Why not?'

He took Quick's empty glass, then smiled at her in a way that made her feel a little floaty. Or maybe that was the two pints of beer she'd already sunk.

'Here you go,' he said, setting another beer on the bar with another of those smiles.

Quick's cheeks heated, even though the room was blissfully air-conditioned. She idly wondered how soon she'd be able to get him back to her hotel. Then she reminded herself that he was barely old enough to be tending bar, and certainly too young for Quick, who was fast approaching thirty and feeling every year of it, particularly after the fruitless heartbreak of this last one. But he was also inhumanly gorgeous, with dark hair and dark eyes, mid-brown skin that shone like gold, and the most alluringly friendly voice Quick had ever heard. It wasn't just his accent, either. Quick had been in South Carolina and its surrounding states for nearly six months now and had developed some immunity to it, but then the bartender looked her right in the eye and called her *sugar*, and she was lost.

Faced with that kind of seductive artillery, any English woman used to stiff upper lips and cold shoulders could be forgiven for melting a little, even one whose resistance hadn't already been shattered by grief.

'Hot out, huh?' he said, smiling again as he leant on the bar.

It was, indeed, hot out. It was the kind of hot that made Quick grateful for chub-rub shorts and breathable cotton, but somehow she didn't think that was what he was talking about.

He gazed at her intently, still smiling that smile, and she gazed right back.

The confidence of the man was infectious.

'Yeah,' she replied dreamily. 'Hot.'

It wasn't her best work, flirting-wise, but then she'd already put in the groundwork. They'd flirted before, though not as intensely as this. The circumstances had been different earlier in the year, but now… Well, now she had nothing left to lose.

Quick hadn't come to Charleston for pleasure. Her best friend had gone missing on a work trip before Christmas, and this bar was one of the few places her bank records confirmed she'd been. Over the past half year, as Quick's search efforts had become more and more impatient, she'd linked up with the families of other missing people and the bar had become ground zero for coordinating the search parties. She'd been here enough times that the guy always recognised her when she walked in, and said, 'Hey, you're back. How are you doing, sugar?' in a way that made her feel completely welcome.

Quick hadn't given him more than casual consideration until now, because she'd been focused on more important things, but now that her money had run out, she'd been forced to abandon her search. She was flying home tomorrow, and she felt like burning some bridges on the way.

The bridge in question leaned over the bar towards Quick, then lowered his voice to say, 'So. What are you doing later?'

Quick laughed. Everything in her life had gone wrong, over and over again, but sometimes things just lined up perfectly. Shame it never happened when it actually mattered.

A patron at the other end of the bar called the beautiful young man away, but he gave Quick a look as he left that told her to stay put, so she did. She paid another server for her shrimp dinner, then sat at the bar playing patience with the deck of cards she always carried in her handbag. She liked the game, despite the unfortunate name, and it had become a frequent habit this year. Tonight, though, on the day before she left the country, the game felt symbolic. It was a way to say farewell to each of the cards before she left her unsuccessful six-month-long mission behind her and retreated back home as a failure.

She shuffled and dealt out the cards on the bar.

King of Clubs, Jensen Mardh.

Three of Hearts, Danny van Brugen.
Eight of Diamonds, Mairead Carlisle.
They hadn't found a single one of them, or any sign of the forty-nine other missing people whose photos and descriptions adorned the cards in the deck.

She dealt them. She flipped them. She built her columns of beautifully descending suits. And then, staring up at her from the latest card she'd turned onto the bar, there was the reason she'd come out here on sabbatical in the first place: *Jack of Spades, Evita Khalyed.*

Quick played one round, then another, and another, but Evita's photo was always a shock when it first appeared, and once her card was face-up, Quick's gaze kept being drawn back to it. She knew it was only her imagination, but the more she played, and the more she drank her beer, the more she felt like Evita's dark eyes were watching her sadly, with disappointment.

Why didn't you find me? Quick could almost hear the straightforward, irritated tone of her voice. *It's only been six months. Are you really giving up so soon?*

'What are these?' the barman asked.

His sudden return made Quick jump, though a decent amount of time must have passed while she was playing and getting lost in her farewells, because there were no other patrons demanding his attention now.

'Cold case cards,' she said, shuffling the pack quickly back together.

'What, now?'

'You haven't heard of them?'

He shrugged and smiled, but then his gaze narrowed on the pack, trying to get a peek as she collected the cards.

'The cold case squads here in the States print them up with details of missing people or unsolved murders,' Quick explained, 'then they give them out to inmates in local prisons. The idea is that one of the prisoners will see someone they recognise, or hear about a case from a cellmate or whatever, and then they'll snitch.'

'Interesting strategy,' he said, plucking the King of Clubs from between her fingers and looking hard at the face of Jensen Mardh.

'This is a special deck we had made,' said Quick uncomfortably. 'You must have heard about all the disappearances in and around Charleston, right?'

The barman furrowed his beautiful unlined brow and shrugged. Apparently he hadn't paid much attention during her previous visits here.

'Well, yeah,' said Quick, taking the King of Clubs back and shuffling it into the pack. 'That's sort of the problem. The missing people are all tourists, most of them moving through Charleston rather than planning to stay here, and no one's found any evidence that anyone's actually been hurt, so there's been hardly any press. But I swear it's happening. People really are going missing. Some of us clubbed together and had these cards made for the local prisons and police departments, trying to get the word out.'

'*Us*?' the barman asked.

'Friends. Relatives. Loved ones of the missing. You know.' Quick tried to order her thoughts at the same time as she shuffled the unruly deck back into a shape that would fit in the card box. 'Thing is, back in December—'

She stopped herself. She didn't want to talk about this tonight. She'd promised herself she wouldn't, that for one night she'd have some fun without thinking about what had happened. It was a downer, and she and the beautiful barman been getting along so well that she didn't want to dampen the mood.

'That's why you're here?' he asked. 'I thought you were just… I don't know. Seeing the sights.'

'Let's not talk about it.' She pasted a smile on her face.

'Okay,' he said, with more readiness than she'd expected. 'Want another beer?'

'Sure,' she replied, glad of the subject change. She'd expected intrusive questions about the things she was trying to forget tonight, but there was none of that from the barman. Probably it came with the job, that pleasant superficiality. When she mentioned Evita, most people wanted to get right into it and start digging, so it was refreshing when he just presented her with a new beer and another of those smiles, then disappeared into the back room to fetch a box of bottles to refill the bar fridges.

Was he closing up?

'Um… Barman?' she called, which felt rude, but she had no idea what else to call him.

'Yeah, sugar?' he replied, emerging with another box.

'I'm sorry, I don't know your name,' she said awkwardly as she got off her barstool.

'Well, Monteiro's my surname,' he said, smiling, 'so everyone just calls me Monty.'

'You can call me Quick.'

His eyes twinkled at her. 'Sounds exciting.'

'It's not.'

He smiled again. God, that smile. Those eyes. And actually, now that Quick came to look at them more closely, those *lips*. She could stare at them for hours. As she watched, he licked them deliberately, and Quick just about melted to the floor.

'I didn't realise how late it was,' she said, picking up her handbag, wondering whether he'd bite. 'I should really go.'

'Why?' Monty asked. 'You got somewhere to be? Got a

boyfriend?'

'Nope,' she laughed. 'But you're casting your net a little narrow, there.'

It took a moment for him to work that one out, then he asked, 'Girlfriend? Other exclusive romantic relationship?'

'Not right now.'

'Then stay,' he said, coming out from behind the bar. 'A friend of mine is having a party tonight at his place, and it's amazing. There's a pool, and this huge old house. Let me finish up here, and we can go together.'

'I don't know, Monty. It's late.'

I'd rather take you back to my hotel, is what she was thinking. She couldn't party all night. She needed to get some sleep, then fly home fresh and sober tomorrow, so she could get back to work the following day. The university had been very understanding about the sabbatical, but they wouldn't keep her position open forever. She needed to show them she hadn't been broken by Evita's disappearance, or she'd risk losing the confidence of the faculty.

But the past six months had been *hard*, hard enough to make her hesitate. She'd had her eye on this beautiful man for months. It was her last night in this beautiful city. Hadn't she earned a night of abandon? Even, perhaps, a one-night stand?

'I'll make it worth your while,' Monty promised, then he leaned down and kissed her.

She was drunk, and she wasn't quite ready, but all things considered it was a pretty good kiss. Good enough that she was willing to put in the effort to try for a better one.

'Just give me five minutes,' he said a little breathlessly. 'Will you wait? Let me settle you down here.'

She hadn't said yes, but somehow she was sitting at a low table by the door in a soft chair, with a beer at her elbow and the buzz of alcohol numbing its way along her veins. She really should say no, but Monty was back behind the bar now, clanking around as he talked to someone on the phone. She couldn't hear the words, but after a moment he raised his voice in a kind of pleading tone that made her feel uncomfortable. He sounded like a kid asking his parents to let him go out and play, which for all she knew could have been exactly what he was doing.

He was *so* young.

Abruptly, Quick didn't want to be here anymore. She gathered her things as quietly as she could, then made her way to the door, but it wouldn't open. She rattled the handle, but it was locked tight.

That was worrying.

Quick started panicking, but she vaguely remembered Monty fiddling around over in that direction as he sat her down. Of course he would have locked up for the night. Perfectly normal. There was nothing weird about that.

He was laughing in the back now, whatever disagreement he'd been having on the phone forgotten, but the incident with the door had made Quick reassess her situation. As he ended the call and swaggered back to the door to fetch her, she was already preparing her excuses.

Then he said, 'Look, I didn't want to say anything and get your hopes up if I'm wrong, but you know the guy on that card?'

'The card?' Quick struggled to pick up his train of thought. 'You mean the King of Clubs?'

'Yeah. Jensen… Jensen whatever.'

'What about him?'

'I think he'll be there. At the party.'

For a moment, Quick thought she'd misheard. 'You *know* Jensen?'

'He's not calling himself that, and I might be wrong, but yeah. I think so. Maybe.'

'Oh my god. I need to call his family.' Quick started fumbling in her handbag for her phone. 'I need to get his mum and—'

'The thing is, I'm not sure,' Monty said, stilling her hands. 'I don't want to get their hopes up, if… Look, just come to the party.' He started guiding her through the restaurant. 'My car's parked out back. I can drive us.'

Quick laughed. She might have been a little drunk, but she wasn't an idiot. She knew she shouldn't get into a car with a virtual stranger, in the middle of the night, in an unfamiliar city from which tourists had been disappearing with shocking regularity over the past six months. She knew it was dangerous.

But then, *Monty* wasn't dangerous. He wasn't just a random stranger, he was the guy who worked at the seafood bar, the same guy she'd seen there every time she'd visited. He had roots in this place.

And Quick knew Jensen's parents. She'd met them, and his sister, and his boyfriend. They'd been one of the most active families in the search party group, working around the clock to find their son, but also never hesitating to contribute their time and support to all the other families who were trying to find their missing loved ones. They were kind, and generous, and so open that the thought of raising their hopes unjustifiably twisted her stomach. Someone needed to check this was real before getting them involved.

But she didn't know exactly where Monty was proposing to take her, and it was late, and she'd already drunk more than enough, and she had a flight to catch tomorrow, and a hangover over the Atlantic would be *brutal*…

Then Monty took her face in his hands and kissed her

again, and she forgot to care.

Maybe she was an idiot after all.

3

KULIKA FOUND JOB Bayly at a beachfront bar in Jamaica overlooking the sunken pirate city of Port Royal. The term *beachfront bar* might conjure up images of white sand and palm trees and sun loungers, but this particular bar was a stark breeze-block box surrounded by rickety metal chairs and tables, set on top of the concrete promontory that reclaimed the edge of old Port Royal from the sea.

Great view, though.

'I wouldn't have thought you'd want to come back here,' Kulika said as she took a seat at the table beside Bayly.

'Wouldn't have thought you would either,' he replied, then he took a long drink from his bottle of beer, his eyes trained on the sunset out over the darkening turquoise water. 'You picked your moment, didn't you? Can't even allow an old sailor a little holiday.'

'You don't get shore leave unless you're sailing, and from what I hear you're not doing much of that these days.'

'And you are, are you?'

'Not unless you call punting on the Cherwell *sailing*.'

'I do not,' Bayly said, looking affronted.

Kulika just laughed. They sat quietly side by side for a

moment as she tried to find the right words to get him to open up, which was always a challenge with Bayly.

'Look,' she said, 'I didn't want to come to the mansion.'

'And I can guess why.'

'You don't have to guess, Bayly. You know.'

'Hmm,' he grunted.

They'd been stuck in that vile place together, at the end. Bayly had made it out before she had. He hadn't come back for her, and she'd never blamed him for that. If she'd got out first, she wouldn't have gone back for him, either.

But now…

She'd done some asking around. She knew Bayly had been living at the mansion for months now, even though he'd always sworn he'd never put down roots on land, not unless someone forced him. And to go back to Bartholomew… Well, that made no sense at all.

'I heard you're living there,' she hazarded.

'Hmm,' he grunted.

'I heard you're running errands in town, like a lackey.'

This time, Bayly made no sound at all, he just stared at the water as though he was out there riding the waves instead of sitting here, baking on the concrete.

'Why are you even involved? That's what I don't understand. You hate him as much as I do. You hate the mansion. You hate dry land. You hate all of it.'

'Maybe,' Bayly hedged. 'But I know enough that I can feel which way the wind is blowing.'

'Don't give me that.'

A kid came out to clear the table and move them on now that the dinner rush was coming in, such as it was. Bayly got a pack of beers to go, then headed down towards the harbour wall to walk along the waterfront. Kulika followed him, though she was sure he'd prefer she didn't. After a few minutes, Bayly cracked a couple of the beers open and handed one to her. They walked for a while in silence, out towards Fort Charles, and Kulika waited. Bayly would talk when he was ready, she knew, and soon enough he was.

'I have someone now,' he said quietly. 'He's involved.'

'How involved?'

'Too involved to come out here with me, even for a day.'

'Fuck. Well, that's not good.'

'And now you're here, getting yourself involved in something I know you'd rather be well clear of, which I'm guessing means that the playboy buccaneer you choose to work for—'

'*Baron* Killian Drake is not a playboy,' Kulika said. Then she thought for a moment and added, 'Anymore.'

Bayly scoffed. '*Killian* now, is it?'

'Yes. It is.'

He scoffed again.

'Come on, Bayly. You, of all people, should understand the need to leave your past where you buried it.'

'Don't know what you're talking about,' Bayly said, taking a swig from his bottle.

'Denial.'

'Says you.' They reached a makeshift bench at the waterfront and Bayly took a seat, putting the cardboard carrier of beer bottles down on the ground at his feet. 'Now,' he said, 'don't you think you'd better tell me what exactly your *baron* thinks you're doing here?'

Kulika sat beside him, stretching her long legs out in front of her in the evening sun. It warmed her in a way the sun in England never seemed to manage, seeping into her joints and sinking into her skin.

'You remember Dr Khalyed,' she said.

'Old Jekyll?' asked Bayly.

'He died.'

'I thought the poison from that lab accident of his killed him decades ago,' said Bayly.

'As it happens, no.'

Bayly sat up a little straighter on the bench. 'But he was a monster. He was biting and killing other Silver. Burning them up to ash.'

'Only because of the way the poison mutated his blood. It wasn't his fault, Bayly. He wasn't a bad man, and he's dead now, anyway.'

'Well,' Bayly said, settling down again. 'Good.'

'Not good, actually. Before he died, someone… else was infected with his blood,' Kulika said, deciding it would be best to leave Jack and the baron's connection to the problem out of it entirely. 'We can cure them, but to do that we need to track down Khalyed's last living human descendant, turn her Silver and use her Silver blood to… I don't know, do something clever and scientific. We've got a team for that. I just need to track the girl down, turn her and get her back to Oxford. As quickly as possible.'

'And that's why you're here?' Bayly asked.

'Yes,' Kulika replied. Then she noted the suspicious look on his face and said, 'You were expecting something else?'

'No,' he said, but he didn't elaborate.

'Her name's Evita Khalyed,' Kulika said, showing the photo on her phone to Bayly. As she did so, she caught a glimpse of Evita's half-there companion and confirmed that she'd been right about the colour of the woman's hair: it was the exact same shade as the fiery reflection of the sunset on the water in the bay.

Bayly looked at the screen for a moment, looked away, looked again, then looked away for good. 'Hmm.'

'Well?' she said. 'Have you seen her?'

'Seen her?' Bayly shook his head. 'She's familiar, perhaps, but then her face isn't unusual. She could be any number of women.'

'But she isn't. That's the point, Bayly: she's the only one of her kind. I need to find her, and her specifically, and I need to do it now. She came to Charleston for a speaking engagement in December, her university says.'

'I wasn't even here in December,' Bayly replied, fixing his gaze back on the waves. 'I came through earlier this year and got… stuck. But not in December. It was just Bartholomew here then. Him and a couple of his pets.'

'That's what I was afraid of.' Kulika sighed. There was no getting around it: she would have to speak to Bartholomew himself, which meant digging up all the memories she'd hoped to keep buried for good. 'The things we did back then, Bayly,' she whispered. 'The things Bartholomew did at Whydah. The things he buried in that mansion.'

'I haven't forgotten,' he said tersely. 'I was thinking maybe you had, if you were planning to go back there.'

'But you've already gone.'

Bayly was quiet for a moment as he finished his bottle of beer, then he put the empty back in the cardboard carrier and screwed the top off another. 'It's too late for me,' he said. 'I don't have a choice anymore. It's not too late for you.'

'I'm not sure I have a choice, either,' Kulika said quietly. 'We've exhausted all our other contacts. We've called in all our favours. This is our last chance.'

Bayly took a long swig of his drink, then he said, 'He won't let you go again, you know.'

This wasn't news to Kulika, but if she acknowledged it then she'd never be able to make herself go back to Charleston, so she pretended she hadn't heard.

'What surname is he going by these days?' she asked.

'Roberts, sometimes. Mostly he doesn't bother with it.'

'Ah,' Kulika said. 'A man who doesn't exist has no need of a name?'

'Precisely.' Bayly finished his bottle in several large swallows, then returned the empty to the box with its friends. 'Returning to the mansion will be… an adjustment.'

Kulika knew what he was saying. The baron was a modern vampire, but Bartholomew was the kind of old school that the modern ones left behind, over time. Baron Drake's mansion and Bartholomew's mansion were separated by more than just the Atlantic Ocean. In terms of their rules and attitudes, they were whole worlds apart.

'It's more crowded than it once was,' Bayly said.

'We've heard rumours,' Kulika replied. There'd been whispers for months about the rising number of new Silver in Charleston, but that wasn't the only spot they'd been multiplying. There had been more in London lately, too, and elsewhere on the continent. All the Silver in the world seemed to be preparing for something, and Kulika had a good idea what it was. 'Bartholomew always wanted to come out of the shadows, didn't he?' she said.

'But your ruler, Solomon,' Bayly said. 'He doesn't.'

'The Primus, you mean,' Kulika corrected him, using his proper title. Solomon was somewhere between a king and a god for the Silver of the UK and beyond, so she wasn't about to go around disrespecting him.

'He'd still prefer we all stayed hidden from humans?' Bayly said, ignoring the correction.

'Until someone forces his hand.'

'Well, that's going to be a problem. Does the Primus know what Bartholomew has been doing? Does he know how many Silver have been turned this year alone?'

A thought occurred to Kulika then. 'Is that why you

thought I was here? To… what? Negotiate an alliance with Bartholomew?'

Bayly shrugged as he twisted the top off his penultimate beer. 'If anyone was going to mutiny against the Primus, it would be your baron,' he said. 'He never took kindly to being ordered. He likes giving orders himself too well.'

'That doesn't mean he's stupid enough to ally himself with a psychopath like Bartholomew.'

'But he *is* stupid enough to send you right back into Bartholomew's cage?'

Kulika couldn't defend Baron Drake without spilling his secrets, secrets that she couldn't trust with Bayly, so instead of replying she sat quietly and finished her beer as the sun dipped beneath the sea.

'They're fishing for them like sharks going after seals,' Bayly murmured into the night. There were no street lamps in this spot, so it was illuminated only by the ambient light from the bar and businesses behind them, and now the moon reflecting off the water. 'Bartholomew's sending all his pets out to pick off the weak ones at the edge of the pack, the ones no one will miss.'

'How many, Bayly?' Kulika asked, wondering what she was about to walk into.

'More than you'd think. He sends the new ones out again when he thinks they're ready, to fetch more, and the new ones… They treat it like a game. They're playing with the humans, romancing them to try to make the turn stick. Then afterwards, when it goes wrong…'

Bayly didn't finish his thought, but he didn't need to. Knowing what went on in that mansion, Kulika could fill in the blanks.

It was old lore, the trick about turning humans Silver by seduction, but it was deeper than the Charleston Silver seemed to appreciate. If you wanted to make absolutely sure that turning a human Silver would actually work, the Silver who turned the human needed to feel some affection for them, and ideally the human should reciprocate that affection. It was connected with frequencies, or absorption rates, or the body's innate ability to heal, or something like that. Kulika had never paid much attention to the science. When Baron Drake had first explained it to her, she'd listened as far as she needed to get the confirmation she'd prayed not to hear: Bartholomew would not have been able to turn her Silver successfully if some part of him hadn't loved her, at least at the start, at least a little.

How much easier it would have been if the truth had been otherwise.

'You're seeing a lot of… failures?' Kulika asked, as delicately as she could.

'Too many.'

'And what's he…?'

'Doing with them?' Bayly laughed darkly. 'Feeding them to the gators.'

Kulika winced.

Until recently, she had never seen the evidence of a failed turning with her own eyes, but now she knew exactly what kind of mindless zombie was created when a Silver tried to turn a human and got it wrong. She also knew from experience that the kindest thing to do for someone in that zombie state was put them out of their misery, and quickly.

Being eaten by alligators did not sound like a quick or merciful death.

'Are you sure about this?' Bayly asked her. 'You're absolutely certain you want to come back?'

Kulika just laughed. Bayly knew as well as she did that she wouldn't even be suggesting a return to the mansion unless it was a last resort.

'It's messy,' said Bayly. 'You know I don't like it when things get messy. It's going to end badly.'

'Then give me another option.'

He looked at her for a moment, then with his gaze fixed back on the water, he screwed the top off the last bottle of beer and handed it to her.

'That's what I thought,' she said quietly.

4

MONTY HADN'T BEEN kidding: the old house did have a pool, and both it and the house itself were enormous.

'My god,' Quick said as she got out of the car and shrugged her handbag onto her shoulder. 'What is this place?'

Monty slammed his door shut and joined her in the darkness. 'It used to be a plantation or something.'

'Oh.' She winced, thinking about how much blood money would have gone into building it. Although Colonial American history wasn't her field of study, she'd read enough on the Elizabethans and the Stuarts to know how the plantations had worked. 'I thought these houses were mostly museums now?'

Monty shrugged and grabbed her hand, then pulled her towards the music that was coming from behind the building. As they approached, Quick was surrounded by an ethereal blue light that cast strange waving patterns onto the canopies of the trees at the back of the property, and onto the Spanish moss that hung from their boughs. It wasn't until they turned the corner that she realised the glow was coming from lights set in the walls of the pool, which refracted through the water in swirling blue patterns to illuminate the back yard. If you could even call something the size of four football pitches a garden.

The space was enormous. In the centre of a large paved area was an Olympic-sized pool, further expanded by the addition of hot tubs and plunge pools and cascading rock-pile waterfalls that surrounded it. A little further out, where the trees and flowerbeds clustered in, there were water lilies and ponds filled with koi carp – god knows how they kept them away from the chlorine – all of which turned the back yard into a kind of grotto. It might have been magical, were it not also heaving with people. There must have been at least two hundred scantily-clad bodies frolicking in the pool, lounging on the benches around it or dancing on the lawn off to one side, where a stack of speakers blared music out across the party.

Within a single second, Quick knew she didn't want to be here. Within two, she was feeling out of place in her floor-length, long-sleeved cotton dress. Within three, she was ready to turn back the way they'd come. She might have done it, too, were it not for Jensen Mardh.

'Monty!' a high voice cried. 'You made it! But you're cutting it fine.' The voice had a British accent, but Quick couldn't pinpoint its source in the crowd.

'Yeah, well,' Monty replied, which gave Quick no information at all.

Then the source of the voice emerged from the mass of bodies chatting and drinking and dancing around the pool, and Quick had a moment's fleeting suspicion that she was being pranked. The woman had hair and skin of a similar colour to Quick's own, but that was where the similarity ended. Where Quick's freckles bunched together across her nose and cheeks as though they were afraid to leave the safety of the herd, this woman's were dusted lightly across her skin with a touch so uniform and delicate that it looked almost artificial. Her hair shone, her nails gleamed, her cheeks pinked attractively with blush instead of burning crimson red like Quick's did. She was wearing a bikini, showing off every curve of her body with a confidence Quick had never managed to embrace, and not a single inch of her looked sunburnt. If she'd been out here all day, then either she had access to the kind of sunscreen Quick could only dream of, or she had magic skin. Seeing her was like being confronted with a vision of everything Quick had the potential to be, if only she didn't insist on being quite so much herself. Unlike Quick, this woman belonged here.

'Well, you might as well join in for the next hour, at least,' the woman said, giving Quick a discouraging look up and down. 'If you're staying, that is.'

'I'm not,' Quick said, at the same time as Monty said, 'We are.'

They looked at each other, while the woman looked at each of them in turn, then Monty said, 'Look, Quick, I told you I'd find your guy if I could, and I will. I just need to go and speak to a friend and find out where he's at, then I'll be right back. In the meantime, why not enjoy yourself? This is Penny. Penny, this is Quick.'

'Quick?' Penny said sceptically.

'Surname,' Quick explained, before turning back to Monty. 'And really, I'd rather just come with you and look, and if he's not here I can call a cab—'

'Five minutes,' Monty said, then he disappeared into the crowd and Quick lost track of him before she could follow.

'Shit,' she murmured.

'Yeah,' agreed Penny, 'he is, sometimes. Hot, though. He's looking for someone for you? Did I hear that right?'

'A friend of a friend. Monty said he'd be here, but I'm starting to wonder if maybe that was a line.' The surroundings weren't filling Quick with confidence. Back at the bar, Monty had seemed like the answer to all her prayers wrapped up in a pretty package, but here amongst his peers he seemed more like a frat boy whose lies were catching up with him. She should never have let him bring her out here in the first place. 'Look, I've got a plane to catch tomorrow. I don't suppose you have the number of a local cab company?'

'You're going home?'

'Yeah. All the way home, ideally.'

Penny looked at Quick more closely and asked, 'Where are you from, exactly?'

'Leicester, originally. You?'

Penny glanced around quickly, then lowered her voice and said, 'I always tell people London, but honestly? Staines.' She smiled, and Quick found herself smiling back. 'Silly, isn't it?' Penny went on. 'Imagine lying about something pointless like that. It seems so immaterial now.'

'Why's that?' Quick asked.

'Oh, you know.' Penny shrugged one shoulder in a shy way that Quick found rather endearing, then she added, 'It's nice to hear a familiar accent. Comforting, you know?'

'How long have you been here?' Quick asked.

'A while,' Penny said. 'Too long, really. But then it's too late to go back now.' Her expression was haunted. It discouraged further questions. Whatever had happened to Penny to keep her from home, it was dark. And for all the superficial decadence of their surroundings, there was a darkness to the party too. It didn't feel like a spontaneous gathering of people who wanted to spend time together. It felt like a group of strangers connected only by their common desire to forget themselves and escape the world outside.

The whole situation made Quick uneasy.

She should just tell Jensen's family about the lead in the morning, and maybe send them out to follow it up themselves in the daylight. Impatient though she was for answers about Jensen's disappearance, which might in turn lead to answers about Evita's disappearance, she was getting a bad feeling about this place, and she'd been through enough that she'd learned to rely on those instincts.

'Anyway,' Penny said, brightening up, 'forget the past. Let's enjoy the *now*, at least until Monty comes back. Did you want to get a drink?'

'I don't think—'

'Come on,' Penny insisted, leading Quick away from the house and around the pool, towards the bar on its far side.

Quick didn't need another drink, but she was certain that Penny needed one even less. As Penny walked across the paving stones on her bare feet, she was weaving in an irregular dancelike motion, out of time with the music and even with her own step. Whatever she had been drinking, she'd clearly already had enough.

'Penny,' Quick said, catching the other woman's hand in her own. 'Do you just want to get out of here?'

'Get out of here?' Penny asked, looking at Quick as though she'd just asked if she wanted to fly to the moon. 'No one leaves the mansion.'

'What do you mean? You absolutely could,' Quick insisted. 'I could call us a car and we could just… go.'

Penny squeezed Quick's hand, then let it go and turned back towards the bar, insisting, 'Just have a drink.'

There was definitely something off about this party. The laughter was too manic, the music was too loud, the expressions around her were too close to crossing over from ecstasy to agony. It occurred to Quick that maybe Penny was trying to take her somewhere quieter, somewhere she could ask for her help. The currently-deserted bar would be a good place for confidences to be shared, so – reluctantly – Quick let herself be led.

The bar was a permanent installation set inside its own powered gazebo. It was a C-shaped structure, marble-topped and brick-built, with cupboards and fridges inside and a tall central plinth ringed with optics and glasses.

'They must throw a lot of parties to need a bar this big,' Quick commented.

Penny didn't reply, she just walked inside the embrace of the gazebo to pour a chilled glass of beer for Quick before shaking up a cocktail for herself, something thick and red that looked fruity and sickly sweet. The glasses were real, which seemed like bad planning at a drunken pool party. When Penny walked back out of the gazebo again and onto the grass, there was a sheen to her eyes that Quick didn't like.

'Are you all right?' Quick asked.

'I haven't been all right for about five months now,' Penny said with a hollow laugh. It was a bleak sound.

'You just look a bit—' Then the light filtering up from the pool hit Penny's face. Quick stared into Penny's eyes for a moment, sure she must be seeing things. But no: there was silver in her eyes. It was like liquid mercury, forming fine silver filaments that followed the path of the tiny blood vessels in the whites of her eyes. 'Your eyes,' Quick said.

'Oh, right.' Penny laughed. 'Yeah, I mean, look around.'

Quick did. At first, she saw nothing, but then she started to spot more glinting eyes across the party, just here and there, perhaps one in every fifteen or twenty of the partygoers.

'Is it drugs?' Quick asked, not having much firsthand

experience to draw upon. Could drugs mess up your eyes like that?

Penny said, 'Something like that.' Then she added darkly, 'You'll see.'

'See what? It's not...' Quick looked down into her drink. 'Is this spiked?'

'No! I only meant that you're here on a kind of important night. You've got about half an hour to make up your mind, but if you decide to stay here with Monty after that... Well, you'll see.'

'See *what*?' Quick asked again, but Penny just sipped at her drink and started moving back towards the pool. 'Look,' Quick said, holding her beer in one hand and fishing in her handbag with the other as she trailed after Penny, 'I only came because Monty said this guy would be here.' She pulled out the missing persons deck, shuffled clumsily through the cards one-handed until she found Jensen Mardh, then held his card up in front of Penny's face. 'His name's Jensen, but Monty said he was calling himself something different. Have you seen him? He's missing.'

'Oh, sweetie, we're all *missing*,' Penny said cryptically, pushing the card away. 'The question is: do you want to be *found*?'

Then she downed her drink, chucked the empty glass onto the grass with an impossibly-long throw, and dived into the pool, leaving Quick alone in the shadows at the far edge of the porch.

For a moment, Quick just stood there, wondering what the hell she was supposed to do now. She could wait for Monty to get back, which seemed increasingly futile, or she could go looking for Jensen herself, which seemed about as promising as waiting for Monty, or she could get out of this unsettling place and try to find some way of calling a cab.

Unfortunately, her phone had no signal, and she was fairly sure that none of the scantily-clad drinkers had theirs to hand right now. That seriously limited her options. She was just contemplating venturing inside the house to see if she could find a landline – the place looked old enough to have one – when the party crowd rippled outwards as though someone had dropped a stone in its centre, then parted to reveal a woman walking towards the steps at the other end of the porch.

Walking wasn't the right word, though. The woman was planting her feet down into the earth as though she was setting her stance for a fight, holding her arms slightly tensed at her sides, poised for action. She reminded Quick of a leopard, all coiled energy and strength, lean muscle and long limbs. She didn't look at all like she was here for the party, and that wasn't just because of her bearing. Not only was she wearing practical clothes – dark jeans, dark boots, sleeveless T-shirt that showed off the natural muscle of her arms – but her expression was focused. One side of her short blonde hair fell over her face, but the side facing Quick was shaved short enough to show her scalp, so Quick could clearly see the look in her eye, and it meant business.

The woman was like a strong breeze blowing in off the river. It took a second or two for Quick to catch her breath.

The woman was heading into the house, and although that had been Quick's destination too, she was absolutely not going to get in her way. Everything about her felt dangerous.

Maybe, Quick decided, she should wait for Monty just a little longer.

5

BARTHOLOMEW WAS HAVING a party.

Kulika shouldn't have been surprised, but it was nearly two in the morning when she and Bayly arrived back at the mansion, and it was a Tuesday night – well, Wednesday morning, now – not the weekend, but the back garden was absolutely heaving. It looked like they were planning to go all night.

'Children,' Bayly muttered under his breath. If it hadn't been for Kulika's Silver hearing, she wouldn't have been able to pick up his words over the thumping music.

'Are these all new Silver?' Kulika asked as she wormed her way through the mass of pulsating bodies. 'This many?'

'No,' Bayly replied.

He wasn't having to push people out of his way; they parted in front of him like water splitting around a rock, then closed up again just in time to rub against Kulika's bare arms. It was making her feel claustrophobic and irritable, and that wasn't a good state of mind in which to walk back into Bartholomew's mansion.

But she could do something about that.

'Move!' she yelled, in the same tone she deployed to bark

orders at the baron's security team back home. It had exactly the desired effect, in that the crowd jumped back and stopped bloody touching her, with the added *undesired* effect that it opened up a clear path between her and Bartholomew, who was leaning just inside the open glass doors that led out onto the porch, speaking with a young man with mid-brown skin and dark hair. When Bartholomew's eyes locked with Kulika's he waved the young man off, despite his protests, and gave her his full attention.

She'd forgotten how imposing he could be. He was tall with soft, tanned skin, long dark hair, and pale eyes that changed their shade to match the sea. He dressed casually, in faded jeans and a dark henley that was unbuttoned just low enough to show a peek of the copper coin he wore on a leather thong around his neck, but his demeanour was far from casual. His face was all hard angles and unyielding edges, his expression cold and avaricious. Perhaps he intended it to be welcoming, but instead he just looked hungry. After all these centuries, he was practically salivating to have Kulika back in his domain.

She almost turned around and left then. The last place in the world she wanted to be right now was here, walking back towards him, but this wasn't just about her anymore. She had the baron to think about, too.

'Kulika,' he whispered, and each syllable felt like a chain wrapping around her throat. 'You're back.'

'Briefly,' she said.

He just smiled, as though she had already surrendered to him, but this time Kulika knew better. She would do a lot of things to save the baron's life, but never *that*.

Bartholomew believed in the power of the written word. Once upon a time, he'd thought the things he wrote could change people's minds, but that belief didn't outlast his transformation into one of the Silver. Now, he just used words to chain people to him, like a devil with a blood-soaked pen. If Kulika gave him the slightest opening, he'd find a way to make her sign her name to his Articles. That would be the end of her freedom, the end of her life, and the end of Baron Drake's too.

Whatever else happened here in these haunted corridors, Kulika Yadav would not sign her life away. Not again.

'I'm looking for someone,' she said. 'She disappeared in your territory at the end of last year. Evita Khalyed, her name is.'

Was Kulika imagining it, or had Bartholomew's composure slipped for a fraction of a second when he'd heard the name?

'I've got a photo,' she pressed on, reaching into her back pocket for her phone. She knew she was rushing this, and probably making a mess of what should have been a delicate negotiation, but if there was any chance that she could get the information she needed and leave without even stepping foot inside the mansion—

'Come in,' Bartholomew said, waving away her phone at the same time as he waved Kulika inside. 'Tell me what you've been doing with your life. Thank you, Bayly. You can go.'

Bayly grunted and turned to leave as ordered, and it was then that Kulika *really* started to worry. Bayly had never been the obedient type. If he was being this compliant, Kulika had to wonder exactly what it was that Bartholomew was holding over him, and how this "someone" of Bayly's was "involved". Bayly had refused to talk about it on the way here, so she could only speculate. She really didn't want to linger long enough to find out the details.

'I'm not staying,' she said.

'I'm sure you have time for one drink,' Bartholomew replied.

He cupped her elbow with his hand to guide her inside, sending shivers of horror over her skin and up the back of her neck. She wanted nothing more than to shrug him off, but that would cause a scene, which was hardly going to get her the information she needed, so instead she bit down her revulsion and let herself be led along the corridor to the other side of the house, then into one of the leather armchairs in Bartholomew's library. She'd been in this room plenty of times before, because it was the place from which Bartholomew ran his empire, but she had rarely been invited to sit. She'd been on her feet, or on her knees, or facedown on the floor, but so rarely in the armchair.

The seat of honour should have made Kulika more comfortable. It did not.

'Have you seen her?' Kulika asked, turning her phone towards Bartholomew once more.

He wasn't sitting. Instead, he closed the door to the room, then leaned against the shelves in a posture that looked relaxed, but felt contrived. It put him above her, over her, peering down at her from a great height.

Just as he always liked to be.

'Rum for you?' he asked, ignoring her phone screen as he pushed off from the shelves and turned to the cupboard where he kept his liquor.

'I don't want a drink, Bartholomew.'

'But you do want my help, Kulika.' He raised his eyebrow at her.

So this is how it would be: she would have to trade a piece of herself for every ounce of cooperation she managed to wring from him. If she'd had time to waste, she might have been able to talk her way to what she wanted without conceding at all, but she couldn't afford to play the long game. In the circumstances, some sacrifice on her part was inevitable. But if she was careful, perhaps she could make it a small one.

'I don't drink hard liquor anymore,' she said.

'Then blood,' he offered.

She swallowed her laugh. She was absolutely not accepting a cup of blood from him, not when she didn't know where it had come from. 'A beer?' she countered.

Bartholomew pressed his lips together, unimpressed. He said, 'Very well.' Then he balled one hand into a fist and, maintaining eye contact with her, slammed it into the wall beside the cupboard, three times, fast.

Kulika heard the footsteps outside immediately, and they were running. When they reached the library door, Bartholomew barked, 'Beer,' then they disappeared back down the corridor again without their owner opening the door, and returned just as quickly as they'd left. The man who let himself into the library was human, surprisingly, and he carried a bottle of beer on a tray next to a chilled glass. As he went to pour it out for her, Kulika saw the black tattoo in the palm of his hand: the mark of Bartholomew's covenant.

She took the bottle quickly from the tray, ignoring the glass. The man bowed and backed out, shutting the door quietly behind him without ever raising his gaze to Bartholomew.

'You have humans sign your Articles now?' Kulika asked once the man's footsteps had rushed away again down the corridor.

'Why not?' he said lightly. 'Those who sail with me have always signed.'

Which was technically true, because all the pirate crews had signed Articles in the old days, but they weren't sailing now, and *the old days* had ended centuries ago. The Articles Bartholomew used now, on dry land, were different. The mark on that man's palm – the one that mimicked the pattern of the copper coin Bartholomew wore at his throat – he gave that only to people he thought were worth binding to his new covenant.

Kulika had worn it, once. To her knowledge, it had never before been tattooed into human flesh, because Bartholomew had never seen any value in humans on land beyond the sustenance of their blood. She had to wonder what had happened to make him change his mind about their worth.

But her curiosity would have to wait. Right now, she needed to be careful how she chose to spend his goodwill, so Kulika just sat and drank her drink. Bartholomew poured himself a rum, leaned against the bookshelves again and drank *his* drink. After maybe a minute had passed in silence, Kulika finally broke it by asking, 'Will you look at the photo?'

'Come now,' Bartholomew replied rebukingly. 'It's been decades since we last spoke.'

'Over a century, in fact.' Which still wasn't long enough for her.

'All the more reason for us to spend some time reacquainting ourselves with each other before turning to business.'

Kulika wanted to say that she had about as much desire to get reacquainted with Bartholomew as she did with the abusive father who'd sold her into marriage in the New World, thus putting her into Bartholomew's path in the first place. But not only would that have been inflammatory, it would also have been untrue. In fact, she'd happily trade the two centuries she'd spent under Bartholomew's flag for ten times that with her father, if only that were an option.

Her father, at least, was dead. With every year that passed, it looked increasingly unlikely that she'd ever be able to say that of Bartholomew.

'I'm not here to talk business,' she said instead.

'Everything is business. Everyone and everything has a price.'

'A woman is *missing*,' Kulika said.

Bartholomew gave her a level look. 'And I'm sure you wouldn't be here searching for her if it wasn't somehow the business of you and your new captain.'

Which, to be fair, was bang on.

'Perhaps we can come to some kind of arrangement,' Bartholomew offered, then he wandered over to his desk in the corner of the room and pulled a large leather-bound book from the top drawer.

He didn't have to tell Kulika what it was; she recognised it well enough. Once upon a time, her name had been between its covers, signed in her own hand and in her own blood: a promise to obey Bartholomew in word and deed, and in heart and soul.

That was his offer, then, for the knowledge Kulika sought.

A small sacrifice indeed.

Bartholomew must have seen the horror on her face, because he said, 'We both know that you wouldn't have come here for any trifling matter, my girl. Whatever this missing woman is to Drake, she must be of paramount importance for him to gamble with his best piece.'

'You don't know what you're talking about,' Kulika said dismissively.

'Don't I? If it were a matter of protocol, he would have sent someone less central to his operations. If it were a matter of force, he would have sent someone he thought could scare me. But instead, he sent the only thing he has to offer that I actually value.' Bartholomew crouched down in front of her with the old book resting on his knees, looking up into her eyes as though he were looking into her soul. 'He sent me *you*.'

Even if Kulika had wanted to reply, her throat was too tight to squeeze out a word. She felt like a fly tangled in a web that spread wider than she'd thought.

'So,' Bartholomew continued, opening the book and turning it so that a fresh new page lay under her hand, 'are we going to talk around in circles all night, or can we just cut to the chase and seal the covenant now?'

'No,' she said, finally finding her voice, though quietly.

'No?' he replied with amusement.

'Never. I will never swear myself to you again.'

He pulled the book back towards himself and snapped it shut before rising to his feet. 'Shame,' he said. 'I thought you wanted to find this missing woman, but if you're sure you can't be persuaded...'

'You *have* seen her, then?'

'Perhaps, perhaps not.'

God, how Kulika wished she could walk away. How she wished she could tell him he was wrong, and that Evita Khalyed was nothing to her, just a random missing woman, not the difference between life and death for the man to whom she owed more favours than she could count.

Instead, she took out her phone again, pulled up the photo and turned it to Bartholomew. 'Which is it?' she asked.

He plucked the phone from her hand and squinted at the photo, as though he were genuinely trying to remember, instead of just leading her on. 'I'll have to think on it,' he said noncommittally, then he disappeared her phone somewhere about his person. 'In the meantime, you must stay. I'll have them make up one of the suites for you upstairs.'

'No, thank you,' Kulika said, putting her half-drunk beer to one side and standing from the armchair. 'I should get going, so if you'll just give me back my phone…'

'Oh, Kulika,' Bartholomew replied with a feral grin. 'You misunderstand me. When I said that you must stay, I meant you truly *must* stay.'

'As your prisoner?'

'As my guest.'

Kulika forced out a laugh, pretending that she wasn't starting to panic. 'You may as well drop the act now, Bartholomew,' she said lightly. 'I'll never give you my oath again. You'll have to take it from me by force, and I warn you: I'm not the same weak, broken lackey who left you a century ago.'

Then his hand was around her neck, her back was against the shelves, and her feet were kicking in the air. She could get out of the hold easily enough, she knew – for all his superhuman strength, she had a measure of her own, along with a whole heap of training – but something was wrong with her throat, and for some reason she couldn't seem to move. Instead of fighting back, she'd frozen in Bartholomew's grip like a kitten held by its scruff in its mother's mouth.

'I won't force the covenant on you,' he whispered against her cheek. 'You know that's not how it works. But however strong you think you've become, you know that I *could*. Soon enough, you'll be begging me to take it from you, just like you did on the *Onslow*. You'll be fighting to get me back under your skin. I *know* you, Kulika. Did you forget that I'm the one who made you who you are today?'

'I'm who I am today in spite of you,' she gasped out, 'not because of you.'

He laughed and let go of her, throwing her back down into the armchair. 'What a tired cliché you've become. You're an empty thing without me. You do realise that, don't you? That void you're trying to fill in the centre of yourself, that thing you've spent the past century searching for, has it not occurred to you that the piece that fits inside that space is *me*? Or are you still in denial about your proper place?'

'You're wrong,' she coughed.

'Denial it is, I see.' He sighed. 'I'd give you the whole world, Kulika. I did, once. He can't give you that.'

'He doesn't have to give me anything. He gave me freedom from you, and that was enough.'

'Until today, when he sent you right back to me.'

There was nothing she could say in the baron's defence that wouldn't make the situation worse, so she said nothing at all as Bartholomew dropped the book back into his desk drawer and slammed it shut.

'If you want information about this missing woman,' he said, 'then you'll stay. Make yourself comfortable. Try to remember why you chose to wear my covenant on your skin in the first place.'

'And if I try to leave?'

'Go, by all means,' he said, smiling that feral smile again, 'if you've decided that she's no longer of any importance to you. But know this: you'll never find her without my help.'

He could be lying. Kulika had seen him lie before, repeatedly and convincingly, but he'd always been honest with her. Unlikely though it sounded, the covenant between the two of them had been one of trust, as well as one of blood. With Kulika, he had always told the truth.

'One night,' she said. 'And only one night.'

'Excellent!' He grinned like a hungry wolf. 'Go on outside. Enjoy the party. You might even like it so much that you decide to stay.'

'I'm leaving tomorrow.'

Bartholomew just continued to grin.

Kulika could only hope that her words would prove as true as his had always been.

6

QUICK STOOD BY the porch as she drank her beer. She was waiting for the beautifully muscled woman who'd gone into the house to come out again, but only so that she herself could slip inside to find a phone. It wasn't that Quick wanted to see her again, to see if she really was as beautifully muscled as she remembered. That would have been ridiculous, because not only was she a complete stranger, in an unfamiliar place, but she was also palpably dangerous.

Quick was just… drinking her beer. Slowly. Once she'd finished it, if the woman still hadn't reappeared, and if there was still no sign of Monty, then she'd just have to go inside and find a phone. And if she happened to bump into the woman while she was in there, maybe that wouldn't be the worst thing in the world.

She'd just about convinced herself that this was the only reasonable course of action when the glass doors opened and the woman stepped outside again. She didn't look happy, her bottom jaw jutting in a way that made it clear she was gritting her teeth. Somehow, that made her even more alluring.

Without conscious thought, Quick took a step towards the

doors, but with her eyes fixed on the woman, she wasn't paying attention to where she was going and barrelled straight into a man coming from the opposite direction.

Her nearly-empty beer glass was knocked from her hand and smashed on the paving slabs, followed by her handbag and all its contents. Her phone skittered across the ground and away into the darkness under the porch, her wallet was kicked between the dancing feet of the partygoers and into the pool, and the cold case playing cards – still loose from their packet – were scattered in a wide circle around her, surrounding her with the faces of all the people she had failed to find.

She had come here for Jensen, she reminded herself with a pang of guilt. *Not to ogle at terrifying yet attractive women.*

She crouched down to collect the cards with new resolve: she would gather them up, track down Monty, get an answer from him about Jensen – one way or another – then get the hell out of here.

'What are these?' asked the man she'd bumped into, crouching down at her side. He looked like one of the buccaneers that Evita had portraits of in her office, with an anchor beard, long chestnut hair and dark lashes framing dark eyes. And he was not happy.

'These?' Quick repeated, still a little dazed from the collision, then she saw that he was holding a couple of the cards between his fingers. 'Oh. These. Playing cards.'

'Why have they got photos on them?' he pressed. 'Why have they got *her* photo on them?'

'They're cold case playing cards,' Quick started to explain. 'They've got pictures of missing people…' Then she saw that the buccaneer was holding Mairead Carlisle's card in his hand. 'You know her?'

'Do *you* know her?' he asked.

'Sort of,' Quick replied. 'I know her family.'

For some reason, that just seemed to make him angrier. Quick was about to enquire further, but Monty chose that moment to finally reappear.

'Monty,' she said, looking up at him, not sure whether or not to be relieved to see him.

'Are you kidding me with this?' the buccaneer asked him, then he grabbed Quick by her arm and hauled her to her feet, making her drop all the cards she'd gathered.

'Hey!' she said.

'With what?' Monty asked the buccaneer. 'What happened?'

'Where have you been?' Quick asked Monty. 'Where's Jensen?'

'Have you seen these?' the buccaneer asked Monty, holding out a handful of the cards.

'Yes,' Monty replied, ignoring Quick entirely.

'Then what the fuck?'

'What?'

'I mean,' the buccaneer said, turning Mairead's card to face Monty, 'what the fuck?'

'So you *do* know her?' Quick asked the buccaneer.

The buccaneer looked at her, then back to Monty, saying, 'Is your girl going to be a problem? Because this,' he picked up a handful of playing cards and broken glass, 'looks like a problem.'

'Jesus, Brandon,' said Penny, coming up behind him. She must have just emerged from the pool, because she was dripping wet and wearing a towel. She unwrapped it from her body to press against the buccaneer's – Brandon's – palm. 'You're fucking bleeding. *Again*. And that's your marked hand.'

'I just want Monty to tell me if this is going to be a

problem,' he said, ignoring Penny and his bleeding hand entirely, as though he didn't even feel it. Quick checked his eyes and saw the same silver in them that she'd seen in Penny's. Maybe whatever they'd taken to make their eyes go like that also made them numb to pain.

And rude.

Monty rolled his eyes and started gathering the cards up himself. 'This isn't going to be a problem,' he said to Brandon.

'I hope not, because I don't want to have to tell Bartholomew—'

'Like he'd ever give you the time of day,' Monty said. 'Let's not forget who was here first, all right? I know what I'm doing.'

'But you've never actually done this before, have you?' Brandon said, glancing at Quick in a way that felt significant.

'Done what?' Quick asked, then she turned to Monty. 'What exactly is going on here?'

But Monty had frozen. He was staring at one of the cards he'd been in the process of gathering up, and he looked like he'd seen a ghost.

The card was Evita's.

'Now you look like he did when he saw Mairead,' Quick said to him, gesturing at Brandon. 'Just how many of the people in this deck do you recognise? And how do you know Evit—'

'Stop,' Monty said, holding up a hand.

'Tell me what you know, Monty,' Quick insisted. 'She's my best friend. You recognised her.'

But Monty just shrugged and said, 'We see a lot of people here.' He had shuffled Evita's card out of sight now, slipping it into the centre of the pack as he snatched the whole lot from the glass on the floor and from Brandon's grip. He moved faster than Quick would have thought possible, if she hadn't just seen it with her own eyes.

'Take her to the block,' Monty said quietly.

'What are you—' Penny and Brandon were holding Quick's upper arms, manhandling her. 'Monty,' she said.

'I'm sorry,' he said quietly, stepping towards her as he slipped her missing persons deck into his pocket. 'This didn't go the way I planned it, but it's the way it's got to be.'

When they were toe to toe, he reached out to touch her face. She thought for a second that he was about to kiss her, so she turned her head to the side, because there was no way she was going to let that happen.

What actually happened was worse.

She should have left when she'd had the chance. If Jensen had ever been here, he was beyond saving, and Penny obviously didn't want to be saved. She was right here, helping Brandon to hold Quick in place with a grip that felt like a vice squeezing tighter and tighter around her arms.

And the woman who walked like she was spoiling for a fight... Well, she wasn't the kind of person who needed saving from anything, but Quick looked around for her desperately, wondering if there was any chance she might be willing to save Quick. From Monty and his friends, from failure, from a life hollowed out by loss after loss, and never filled up again.

Too late now.

Monty's hand covered Quick's nose and mouth, then his teeth found her neck. If she could have breathed, she might have screamed. She did neither.

In her last moments of consciousness, as her vision dimmed, she thought she caught a glimpse of sunshine in the darkness. The pain faded into panic, and panic faded into

nothing at all.
Just emptiness and cold.

7

KULIKA STEPPED OUT onto the porch and into the night air with a measure of relief, but no pleasure. Then Bayly joined her, and her discomfort flared into irritation.

'You didn't tell me it had got this bad,' she said accusingly. 'What's going on here, Bayly? This party, the pool, all these people, and don't think I didn't notice those new buildings over on the far side of the property. What are they? Dorms? And you let me walk in here without warning me that he's marking humans now. *Why* is he marking humans?'

Bayly didn't reply to any of this, he just stood beside her as the two of them looked out across what had once been the dirt training ground on which they'd wrestled, and was now a pool party filled with teenagers and twenty-somethings. It had been important, that space. Back in the day, they'd established the pecking order of the mansion on that dirt. The better you fought, whether clean or dirty, the higher your rank in Bartholomew's crew. It looked as though those days were long gone. Now, Bartholomew's followers seemed to be establishing their hierarchy through drinking games, wet T-shirt contests and drunken brawls.

Maybe that wasn't such a change. After all, they had been pirates, once.

A splash of ethereal colour drew Kulika's gaze to the far side of the porch. There was a group of four people there, two men and two women, standing apart from the rest of the party. The colour she'd seen was the red hair of one of the women, shining like fire in the dark. Kulika caught only a glimpse of her soft face, transformed into an eerie kind of beauty by the undulating light filtering up through the pool, before she walked away arm-in-arm with her friends, crossing the grass towards the new modern block that lurked beyond the trees.

Her hair shone like sunset on the water. Like the hair of the woman who was standing in the photograph next to Evita Khalyed.

'Who's that?' Kulika asked Bayly, but Bartholomew was the one who answered. She hadn't realised he was there, but then he always had been beyond-supernaturally stealthy. She would have to remember that, along with so many other things that she had hoped could stay forgotten.

'The redhead?' Bartholomew asked. 'If you want her, she's yours.'

'All I have to do is sign, right?' Kulika scoffed.

Bartholomew just smiled. Kulika turned back to Bayly, meaning to ignore Bartholomew, but Bayly had already slipped away.

Lucky him.

'She's a person, not your property,' Kulika said, turning back to Bartholomew.

'She's both,' he replied. 'She took the deal: we turned her Silver and she signed the Articles. She wears the mark of my covenant. If you want, I can have her in your bed within the hour, ready and waiting.'

'Aside from the obvious objections,' Kulika said, putting herself between Bartholomew and the retreating vision of the woman with the sunset hair, 'do you really mean to convince me to sign your Articles by gifting me a woman who's made herself your property by doing exactly that? You're not going to tempt me into slavery by offering me one of your slaves.'

'Not slavery, Kulika,' he said, reaching out to caress her cheek. She caught his wrist before he could touch her skin, tossing his hand away, and he laughed. How he loved to laugh. 'You are not her,' he whispered, leaning in closer than she would have liked. 'The terms of our covenant would be different.'

'Different how?'

'Better. For you, that is. Worse, for me. I'd do that for you, Kulika. That's how much it would mean to me to have you return home, my prodigal daughter.'

It was true that Bartholomew had been like a father to her three hundred years ago, but by the authoritarian standards of the time, it was a hollow title.

'This isn't my home,' she said. 'It never was.'

Bartholomew looked like he was about to make her another offer, but then the young man who'd been trying to speak to him earlier returned, saying, 'Sir, I'm sorry, but—'

'You'll be sorrier in a moment, Mr Monteiro.'

'Sir, please, I wouldn't interrupt if it wasn't important. It's just that…' The young man glanced at Kulika, then looked back to Bartholomew. 'Sir, I really need to speak with you. *In private.*'

Bartholomew glared at the poor kid for a moment, then turned to Kulika and waved her off into the party, saying, 'I'll catch up with you later. In the meantime, feel free to make whatever enquiries you like of my guests.'

Which was as good a suggestion as any, she supposed, but she wasn't likely to get very far without her phone and the photo of Evita Khalyed that it contained. She wasn't likely to get anywhere at all without Bartholomew's cooperation. He'd recognised the woman's face, Kulika was certain. He knew her, or had seen her at least, but he wasn't going to give up that information easily. Maybe, between now and the morning, she could come up with some way to bargain it out of him. Maybe she could track down Bayly and get him to explain exactly what plan of Bartholomew's required this many new Silver and humans carrying Bartholomew's black mark. Or maybe she'd be better off getting out of here right now, before the water got too deep for her to stand in it.

She stepped off the porch towards the pool, meaning to find some answers, but slowed as she heard the young man start talking to Bartholomew behind her.

'Sir, we've got a problem,' he said.

'Then deal with it, kid,' Bartholomew replied.

'It's about the girl I brought in tonight. She's being… uncooperative.'

'And whose fault is that, hmm?'

Kulika's hearing had improved since she'd left Bartholomew. Either he'd not considered the fact that the abilities of the Silver improved with age, or he'd underestimated the effect that a century would have on hers, because he didn't make any attempt to move their conversation further into the house.

'Surely by now you know not to bring someone new so late in the cycle,' he continued. 'Just let her go.'

'That's the problem, sir. I can't.'

'And why not?'

'The thing is, the reason I brought her in the first place was that she was looking for some of the people who've gone missing, and it seemed like the fewer questions there were the better, you know? But it turns out there's a whole bunch of families looking for a whole bunch of missing people, and she had these and—'

Kulika peeked over her shoulder just in time to see the kid handing a stack of small cards to Bartholomew, who began to leaf through them.

'And what exactly are these?'

'Missing person playing cards, she says. The thing is, sir, if you look at the card on the top of the pack…'

Bartholomew flipped the card so he could see its face, then he became very still indeed. From this angle, Kulika couldn't see anything except the back of the card.

'She was looking for Jensen,' the kid said. 'But she said this name, and I think… I think she knows Jane.'

Bartholomew looked up, in what appeared to be shock. As he did so, he noticed Kulika's attention and realised his mistake. He nodded her an irritated farewell, then drew the young man back into the house and out of earshot.

Shame. He wouldn't underestimate her so easily next time.

But the endeavour hadn't been entirely fruitless. She had more information now than she'd had at the beginning of the night. She was more convinced than ever that Evita Khalyed was here, or had been here, and it sounded like she was just one of many. Mr Monteiro had spoken about *the missing people* as though there were a lot of them, maybe enough to fill a whole deck of cards. On top of that, there was one that was important to Bartholomew, important enough to drag him away from tormenting Kulika.

Jane.

His reaction to that name, to the picture on that last card… Maybe that was something Kulika could leverage to get the information she needed. If only she could get her hands on those cards.

First, though, she needed to find Bayly and make him spit out some answers.

She waded out into the party, letting the conversation flow over her. Drinks. Hook ups. Fights. Drugs. Competitions between all the young idiots to see who was the strongest, even though they all now had more strength than they could wield responsibly. What on earth was Bartholomew thinking? There was a reason that the Silver were turned slowly, one by one, then ushered gently and carefully into immortality under the supervision of their creators and elders. This kind of mass expansion meant that there were precious few experienced Silver to guide them through the transition, or to curb their excesses when they stepped out of line. If a bunch of them all decided to go rogue at once…

Kulika felt like she was walking into a powder keg with a fuse of indeterminate length. There was no telling when it might go off. The only sure thing was that, sooner or later, it would.

8

WHEN QUICK WOKE up, her tongue felt fuzzy in her mouth, her throat was dry and her back ached. Sitting up was an effort. It was dark, or near enough. There was a faint light seeping through a long, straight crack in the ceiling above her, but not enough to fully illuminate the space she was in: a rectangular room about twenty feet wide with a low ceiling, no windows and a dirt floor. A cellar, then. It smelled damp and vegetal, and she could hear a drip echoing from what sounded like a long way off. Beyond that sound, there was nothing.

No birdsong. No traffic. No thumping party music.

The world had been taken away.

Then her ears popped and she heard a noise that made her jump back against the wall: the scuffling sound of feet on dirt. There was someone, or something, in here with her.

'Are you still human?' a voice asked from the darkness at the far end of the cellar. Feminine, North American accent, but not local.

Quick wasn't sure whether to be relieved or concerned to have company. And the question was... odd.

'Excuse me?' Quick replied with a dry voice that broke

into a whisper.

'Human,' the voice said, but this time it was quieter, as though the word had been spoken in the opposite direction.

'What do you mean *human*?' Quick asked. 'What else would I be? And who are you? And where are we? And what the fuck?'

'That about sums it up. You want water? There're faucets in the corner over here.'

Abruptly, Quick realised that she was parched. But she was also wary of the voice luring her into the darkness, and aware that the person who owned it had yet to answer any of her questions.

Quick stood with difficulty, and not just because she was feeling unsteady. She was five foot nine and her head was grazing the ceiling, even though her feet were bare. Who knew where her sandals had gone, or her handbag.

Then she remembered: the missing person playing cards, Brandon and Penny holding her arms, Monty leaning down and biting—

Her hand flew to her neck. She could feel the tender wounds there, scabbed with dried blood.

'He bit me,' she said in disbelief.

'Yeah, the vampires do that,' the voice said. 'Just be grateful you're not a zombie.' Then its owner walked into the faint light leaching through the crack in the ceiling. She looked like Lara Croft after she'd fought her way out of a particularly filthy tomb, only she had light brown skin, bleached blonde hair with long black roots, chipped silver nails and a nervous energy that gave Quick the impression that she was both unpredictable and unsafe to be around.

'Excuse me?' Quick asked politely, wondering how far she'd get if she started running. The room felt big, but there was no guarantee she'd be able to find a way out of it. She couldn't run forever, and likely not long at all in this dehydrated state.

'You said you got bitten,' the woman said.

'Yes,' Quick replied tentatively.

'Show me your eyes.'

Quick backed away as the woman stepped closer.

'I will pin you down and pull your eyelids up myself if you make me,' the woman growled.

'Jesus, Xiaoyu,' said another voice from the shadows, then a young man was standing at the woman's side, tugging her back by the arm. He was tall and gangly, hunched over in the low space, with dark skin and a scraggly little beard that made Quick think he was probably younger than he looked. She couldn't place his accent, but it wasn't purely American; there was at least a bit of French in there. 'She just woke up,' he said. 'Give her a chance.'

'A chance to murder us all?'

'All?' Quick asked, looking between the two of them. 'How many of you are there?'

There was a click and suddenly the room was flooded with light. Quick had to look away, blinking the strobing brightness out of her eyes for a few seconds before she could bear to look back. When she did, she saw that the room was much larger than she'd first imagined, stretching easily a hundred feet away from her, supported at regular intervals by concrete pillars. Breeze-block walls. The far corner had been screened off with ratty sheets hanging between the pillars. It was clearly some kind of flood cellar, but it looked like an unusually low parking garage, lit at irregular intervals by fluorescent strips across the concrete ceiling.

Quick's side of the space was empty except for her, Xiaoyu and the young man, but the other side was a patchwork of people laid out on makeshift beds on the dirt floor, mostly fashioned from blankets and clothing. There must have been a hundred people down here, easily, and every single one of them was looking at her.

'We watch,' the young man explained. 'When they open the hatch and throw someone down,' he said, indicating the space on the ceiling where the line of light had now disappeared in the glare of the fluorescents, 'we turn out the lights and we wait to see what wakes up.'

Which explained why everything had been so silent when Quick opened her eyes. The people in the cellar hadn't been sleeping. They'd been keeping guard.

'And now I need to see your eyes,' Xiaoyu said, then she grabbed Quick by the hair and dragged her directly under one of the fluorescents. Quick yelled and elbowed back, but by the time she'd started fighting in earnest, Xiaoyu had already let her go. Quick ended up flailing into an undignified heap on the floor.

'She's clean,' Xiaoyu declared.

Only then did the people watching from the other side of the cellar make a sound, as though they had been collectively holding their breath until that moment.

'Louis,' the young man said, holding out his hand to Quick. She shook it without thinking, because it was just what you did. 'I'd say *welcome*, but…'

Quick looked at him, at Xiaoyu, and at the hundred-odd people beyond them. They were diverse in appearance but mostly young, either teenagers or kids in their twenties. There were some older adults in the mix too, but none of them looked older than fifty. A few were looking at her with curiosity, but most of them had lost interest now that the excitement was over.

'You were looking for the silver,' Quick said as she put it together. 'Weren't you?' she asked Xiaoyu. 'You were looking for silver in the whites of my eyes.'

'You noticed they have that, huh?' Xiaoyu jutted her hip out to one side and rested her hand on it, a gesture that was more cocky than sassy. She was clearly the one calling the shots in this hole in the ground.

'So it *is* drugs, then?' Quick asked.

'Drugs?' Xiaoyu laughed dismissively. 'What drugs do you know that make your eyes go weird, give you super speed, super hearing and super strength, make you immortal and give you a thirst for human blood? Come on.'

'But…' Quick said. 'You mean you were serious about the vampires?'

'You got bitten and you still don't believe me?'

'No. Yes. I don't know. *Vampires*?'

'Look,' Louis interrupted, 'this is going to be a long conversation, and I can't stand all hunched up like this forever, so can we get away from this damned hatch and sit down?'

Xiaoyu glanced up at the covered hole above their heads then started backing up towards the far side of the room. 'Right,' she said. 'The night's not over yet. There could be more.'

'More what?' Quick asked.

'Just…' Xiaoyu glanced up, then away, then up again, getting jittery now. It looked like her anxiety was back, and then some. 'Just get away from the fucking hatch, okay?'

They'd barely taken a step when there was a *clank* from right above their heads. Neither Xiaoyu nor Louis said anything, they just grabbed Quick by the arms – still tender from Brandon and Penny's manhandling – and dragged her to the far side of the cellar in a crouched and panicked run, coming to rest behind a pillar about halfway along the space.

Louis pressed a finger to his lips, then the lights went out.

The clanking came again, followed by the rasp of something hard scraping across the floor above, then the hatch was lifted open. Quick peeked around the corner of the pillar as a square of warm light shone down onto the dirt floor below, bringing with it the sound of conversation.

'You're zero for five,' a man said, braying so loudly that this words were clear to Quick even though she was some distance from the hatch. 'When are you going to call it quits? None of these girls fancy you, Bub. Give up already.'

'Right, yeah,' came the reply, 'and remind me, what are you on? One for seven? Doesn't seem to me like you're doing much better.'

'Um, hello? I have *one*, at least. You got none, buddy. None.'

'Yet,' the second speaker said. Then, as if to punctuate his speech, a bundle of something person-sized – probably a person, Quick forced herself to admit – dropped through the hatch and onto the cellar's dirt floor with a sickening, cracking crunch. The hatch shut a second later, blocking out the conversation from above and leaving them in the darkness. Her eyes had become accustomed to the brief light, so now Quick couldn't see a thing, but she could feel the reassuring press of concrete at her back, and the warmth of Xiaoyu and Louis pressed on either side of her.

'What now?' Quick whispered.

'Now we wait to see what they turn into,' Louis whispered back.

'You mean they could turn into a vampire?' Quick said, horrified. Then the implications filtered through her panic and she clapped her hand to her neck. 'Am *I* going to turn into a vampire?'

'If you haven't yet, then you won't,' Louis said. 'And you haven't, because there's no silver in your eyes. It shines like crazy under those fluorescents, and yours didn't. You're clear. You're no vampire, I promise. Going by what they were just saying, though, this latest one's going to turn, one way or another.'

'And most of the time they go quickly,' Xiaoyu muttered quietly. 'So shut up and watch.'

Quick wanted to ask more, but Xiaoyu shushed her down before she could get the words out, so instead she sat between them in the darkness and peered around the pillar, waiting for her eyes to acclimatise again. By the time they did, the bundle underneath the tiny crack of light coming through the ceiling was starting to move.

There was a stomach-churning *snap* and everything was suddenly utterly silent. Where Quick's arm pressed against Xiaoyu's side, she could feel Xiaoyu's heartbeat thumping against her ribcage, but she couldn't hear her breathing. It felt like the whole room was holding its breath, unbidden, as though this were a practised routine.

Except the person who had fallen through the hatch. There was a loud, rasping breath coming from that direction now. It had an unpleasant, gurgling quality to it that made Quick think of the last drops at the bottom of a milkshake. The person didn't move, though. Not at first. To begin with, they just gurgled and sniffed. The noise lasted long enough to make Quick uncomfortable, because surely they should be going to help the poor person if they'd hurt themselves falling into the cellar, shouldn't they? It sounded worryingly like they might have punctured a lung, and if that was the case then shouldn't they be putting them on their side or doing something to help them breathe before they drowned in their own blood?

Quick opened her mouth to suggest this, but she only managed to say, 'Shouldn't—' before the person beneath the hatch snapped their head up from the ground. Their face was snarling, twisted and feral, and they were looking directly at Quick.

'Idiot,' Xiaoyu muttered, then she scrambled to her feet and yelled, 'Blankets! Back to row three, ready to bundle on my mark!'

'Run!' Louis said to Quick, so she did, following Xiaoyu to the far side of the cellar, where people were already on their feet and lining up between the columns across the width of the space, holding out coats and blankets and sheets between them. Louis and Quick squeezed between two people to get behind the line, then turned in time to see the figure under the hatch rising unsteadily to their feet.

It was a white man, Quick thought, though with the dirt, loose clothes, twisted features and mid-length hair falling over his face, it was difficult to be sure. He was tall, too tall to stand upright in the cellar without bending over, but he didn't even try to reach his full height. Instead, he held his body in a poised, forward-leaning stance, back hunched and arms hanging down loosely from his shoulders. When he raised his head, his attention snapped to the blankets and he started to move towards the crowd, slowly at first, then quicker, until he was running full pelt at them with an inhuman, guttural roar.

'Lights!' Xiaoyu yelled, and the fluorescents snapped on.

The man screamed, losing momentum and direction as he ploughed into the blanket fence and was bundled up like a burrito. But he recovered quickly, too quickly, his limbs flailing free of their constraints and taking out several of the people who were trying to pin him. Quick lunged into the fray without thinking, grappling to snatch a piece of the blanket and secure it around his arms.

'Mind his mouth!' someone yelled, too late. The man's

teeth had already sunk into Quick's forearm.

She screamed – this was fifty times more painful than it had been when Monty bit her – then she started pounding him around the head with her other fist until, finally, his jaw released its grip. The release was abrupt enough to take her off balance, toppling her down on top of him as she wrestled to get the blanket over his head. He pinned her, his grotesquely twisted face snarling inches from her throat as the others held him back.

No, she decided.

The panic flowed out of her body, replaced with a calm sense of purpose. Leveraging her not-inconsiderable weight against his, she flipped him, then straddled his body with her knees on his shoulders, forcing his back to the ground. She reached for a nearby blanket and bundled it around his head so he wouldn't be able to bite again, then it was just a matter of holding him in place while the others got him wrapped up tight.

'Knock him out!' Xiaoyu yelled.

A big white guy who looked like a football player raised his fist above the snarling man's swaddled head, then brought it down with a force Quick hadn't managed herself. Suddenly, the bundle went still.

For a moment, Quick just sat there in shock, then Louis came up behind her, helping her off the man and to her feet.

'Zombie,' he explained.

'Zombie,' Quick repeated, numbly.

'It happens sometimes,' he said. 'When they try to turn one of us into a vampire and it doesn't take, this is what you get.'

'Oh no,' Quick said, looking with horror at the unconscious creature at her feet, at the bite on her arm, then feeling for the crusted bite at her neck. 'Please tell me I'm not going to—'

'Relax,' Xiaoyu said. 'Zombie-ism isn't catching, and I already told you the vamps didn't try to turn you. One of them just drank from you a bit. No big deal.'

'No big deal?' Quick was reeling. 'I just got bitten by a zombie, and found out Monty's a vampire—'

'They call themselves the Silver,' Louis chimed in unhelpfully.

'—and that he drank my blood, and it's *no big deal*?'

Xiaoyu pulled aside her shirt collar, displaying a roadmap of scars and half-healed scabs snaking down her neck and onto her shoulder. 'Yeah,' she said. 'No big deal. Why else do you think they keep us down here? We're the blood bank. Stop being such a fucking drama queen about it.' Then she grabbed the unconscious zombie by one ankle while another woman grabbed his other, and together the two of them dragged him back towards the hatch.

'Don't mind Xiaoyu,' Louis said, kneeling at her side to spare his back. 'She's been here longer than most of us. A lot of people die in this place. It hardens you up, you know?'

'How long?'

Louis shrugged. 'I don't know. Months? I've been here since March, and Xiaoyu'd already been here a long while before then.'

Months.

Quick remembered the way Monty had frozen when he'd seen Evita's face on that card, and the way he'd shut Quick down when she'd tried to say her name. He'd recognised her, or her name. And if he knew her, then maybe…

'My best friend has been missing since December,' Quick said. 'I came here looking for answers about another missing person, then I thought I was onto a lead about my friend, but the moment I started to ask around at the party—'

'You ended up here,' Louis finished for her.

Which was exactly where Evita could have ended up.

'Evita Khalyed,' Quick said. 'Do you know the name?'

Louis shook his head.

'Evita Khalyed,' Quick said again, raising her voice as she looked at every face in the cellar, one by one. Between the panic and the zombie and the shock, she hadn't been paying attention to them earlier. She might have missed her friend in the crowd. The hope surged in her chest like a hot, sharp splinter of desperation. 'Evita Khalyed! Are you here?'

'Keep your voice down!' Xiaoyu whisper-yelled at her. 'They can hear you upstairs.'

'They have their dorms up there,' Louis said. 'If they think you're causing trouble…'

'This place is like cold storage,' muttered a man behind her. 'We're fast food. Disposable.'

'Has a woman called Evita been through here?' Quick asked him.

'No Evitas,' Xiaoyu said, as though that were the end of the conversation. She and the other woman had reached the hatch now, and they unceremoniously dumped the zombie underneath it.

Quick looked around, appealing to the rest of the crowd as she said, more quietly this time, 'Has anyone else met an Evita here?'

'No,' Xiaoyu said. 'They haven't.'

'Why don't you let them speak for themselves?' Quick snapped back.

'Why don't you try using your brain, noob? Far as I know, I was the first one they put down here, so if I don't know Evita, no one else will either. Now shut up while I get rid of this guy.'

Then she reached up and thumped on the hatch with her

fist.

'Jonah! You're zero for six,' she yelled. 'Jonah! Come and clean up your own damn mess!'

The hatch opened wide and Xiaoyu took a few big steps back.

'You want to be number seven?' said a man from above, one of the same voices from earlier.

'Fuck off, kid,' Xiaoyu spat. 'And if you don't want your blood supply to dry up, maybe you could try feeding us, huh?'

Instead of answering her, he jumped into the cellar, scooped the unconscious zombie up into his arms, then leapt back out again in a single bound. If everything that had happened that evening up until this point hadn't already convinced her of the truth, that simple physical impossibility put it beyond question. These people were not human.

The hatch thumped down again, sealing Quick and the other prisoners into the vampires' larder.

'What will they do with him?' Quick asked Louis.

'I don't know,' he murmured. 'And I'm pretty sure I don't want to either.'

It was only then that Quick's adrenaline wore off enough for her to feel the pain in her arm. She winced.

'Let's get that clean,' Louis said, standing into his hunched crouch as he led her through the drift of blankets to the corner of the cellar that had been sectioned off from the rest with hanging sheets. Quick had expected some kind of praise or thanks for her bravery with the zombie, because she had literally thrown herself into danger to help the others, but most of the cellar inhabitants barely looked at her. Like Louis had said, being down here seemed to harden people up, as though they'd grown protective shells over their feelings.

'Friendly bunch,' Quick murmured.

'Don't judge them too harshly,' Louis replied softly. 'The truth is, people don't last long down here. You don't tend to make friends, because you'll only lose them.'

'You're friendly,' Quick pointed out.

'Well, look out for yourself and don't make me regret it. Through here,' he said, ushering her around the corner.

There was a line of stainless steel sinks, a couple of shower heads set in the wall above a drain in the middle of a small concrete area of flooring, and a couple of grungy-looking steel toilet cubicles. Louis helped her wash the wound as clean as they could get it in one of the sinks – which wasn't as clean as Quick would have liked – then bind it up with a strip of cotton torn from the sleeve of her dress.

'Right now, it's the most sanitary thing down here,' said Louis apologetically as he ripped it into pieces. 'Sometimes they let us shower and change clothes when they take us up to feed, so hopefully someone will bandage this up for you properly then.'

'When's that likely to be?' Quick asked, desperate to get out of the cellar, but none too keen to get bitten for the third time in as many hours.

Louis just shrugged.

'Xiaoyu was right under that hatch when the vampire opened it,' Quick said quietly, trying to understand the strange dynamic between her and the one she'd called Jonah.

'Yeah,' Louis replied.

'But we were all clearing away from the hatch earlier.'

'Because of the zombie. The vampires are bad, but they're rational, and they need us alive for our blood. The zombies are bad too, but they're pretty easy to take down if we work together, like you saw. The problem is that sometimes the vampires do manage to turn someone into one of them, and when those wake up down here all blood-starved and crazy… Well, that's the scary shit. That's when people die.'

'But if the newly-turned ones are so dangerous, and the vampires care so much about keeping us alive, why do they put them down here?'

'Because feeding them is what we're for,' Louis said darkly. 'That's *why* they want to keep us alive. If we die doing it… Well, to them, that's a fair trade.'

'Lights out,' said Xiaoyu from beyond the bathroom curtains. 'Let's all get some sleep while we can. I'll watch the hatch with Reynolds.'

Louis rushed Quick back out into the main cellar, settling them both onto a blanket on the floor as the room plunged into darkness once more. Quick should sleep, she knew, because if today was any indication of what was to come, she'd need to be well-rested for tomorrow.

Instead, she opened her eyes into the dark cellar and replayed the moment the zombie had pinned her to the dirt and snarled into her face. Over and over again.

She was going to die down here, and there was not a person in the world outside this hell hole who knew where she was.

9

KULIKA HADN'T BEEN able to find Bayly that night. She'd thoroughly searched the party and the mansion before following his scent to the parking area out front, where it disappeared. The traitor had driven away and left her here.

By that time, it had been late enough that Kulika would normally have been getting up for her dawn training session, but between the jet lag, the all-nighter and the nocturnal hours they kept at the mansion, she'd decided to pack it in and go to bed instead. That was when she'd discovered that the suite that had been prepared for her was not only one of the grandest in the house, it was also the suite neighbouring Bartholomew's.

His and hers.

Kulika couldn't imagine what Bartholomew thought he was playing at. There'd never been anything romantic between the two of them; he was a paternal figure to Kulika, quite apart from the fact that she was gay, and he had been celibate since the sixteenth century. It was inconceivable that he had carnal designs on her, which could only mean that he wanted her under his control in other ways.

For Bartholomew, that was not out of character.

As a general rule, control freaks didn't make good pirate captains, but Bartholomew was the exception to that rule. Piracy was supposed to be a democratic institution, as set out in the common Articles.

ARTICLE I. Every man shall have an equal vote in affairs of moment.

There was a share of the loot for each man according to his contribution, there was compensation paid to those who were injured during the course of their duties, and there were harsh penalties for those who broke faith with their crewmates. That was how the Articles had started out: as a code of conduct to govern buccaneer – and later pirate – civilisation. They weren't intended as chains to wrap around the crew, to twist them and press them into committing horrific depravities, all in the name of loyalty to their captain, to the exclusion of all others. Piracy was supposed to be about freedom, not cultism.

Bartholomew did things differently.

If it had been anyone else wearing the fancy hat, the crew would have mutinied, but Bartholomew wasn't just anyone. He'd always had that intensity about him, too unsettling to be called charisma and too intriguing to be repellent. The balance had been different at the beginning, when Kulika had first been thrown into his orbit. Now she felt more horror and less awe. Still, even she had to admit that there was an undeniable majesty in the dramatic way he burned the world down. Part of her understood why so many people had gathered to watch, then and now. What she couldn't understand was why Bartholomew was so keen for her to be amongst their number.

She was contemplating this mystery as she lay in the four-poster bed she'd been allocated, fully-clothed and unwilling to let her guard down enough to do anything about that, staring at the canopy above her head. It was fitted with mosquito netting to keep out the worst of the bugs that congregated on the marshy areas of the property that slipped down towards the Cooper River, but to Kulika it just looked like a spider trap. She imagined them all up there, spinning their webs and multiplying in the dark, waiting for the right moment to strike, just like the Silver of Bartholomew's mansion.

She must have dozed a little, because she was jerked awake by a knock next door, muffled voices, footsteps running, smashed glass and yells. She went from sleeping to awake to out of the door within a second.

'What?' she asked Bartholomew as he hurried past along the corridor, pulling a henley on over his head.

'Go back to bed, Kulika.' He headed down the wide, curving staircase without stopping. A human woman was at his heels, rushing to keep up. 'How far out are they?' Bartholomew asked the human as he descended one flight and made for the next.

'Ten hours, they say,' she replied.

'Ten *hours*? Where the hell are they?'

'Oklahoma, sir.'

'Well, get Jessamy back on the phone now. They definitely have the footage?'

'And the bodies, sir.'

'Good. It's time to put out the call.'

'Yes, sir. All of them?'

'All of them,' he said. 'I want them here on Sunday, after we've finished this cycle. The last cycle.'

Then Kulika didn't hear anything more, but she had a bad feeling. Whatever it was that Bartholomew was planning to do here with all these new Silver, it was starting now.

She quietly closed her bedroom door behind her and

headed down the stairs after Bartholomew, moving as silently as she could. She followed the sound of his voice to the back of the house, past the library, through the old kitchen to the door that led down to the wine cellar. It was shut, and there were two Silver standing guard beside it.

Then a voice from beyond the door called, 'I can hear you out there, Kulika. Go back to bed.'

So much for her attempts at subterfuge. He wouldn't say a thing while she was standing out here, so she decided to take her snooping elsewhere. Maybe she'd find a lead from somewhere – or someone – else on the property.

She passed the library on her way back to her rooms, then quickly doubled back as she realised it was open, and unoccupied. With Bartholomew shut away downstairs, she couldn't imagine a better opportunity to go through his private sanctuary, so before she could think too hard about everything that might go wrong, she slipped inside and closed the door silently behind her.

The shelves and cupboards were a waste of time, and she quickly discounted them as containing only books and booze and memorabilia from their old days on the high seas. His desk, though. That was where he'd always kept his secrets.

The leather-bound book was in there, of course. That was no surprise. The shock was the number of new signatures that Bartholomew had accumulated since Kulika left. If her quick count was correct, and assuming all the recent signatures were of Silver who were still alive and serving him, then he already had an army. There were hundreds of names in that book, all drawn in the blood of the signatories, reeking of death and rot. If Bartholomew chose to marshal them all for whatever insurgent purposes he had in mind, then with the power even a new Silver had in their body, that many of them collected together would leave nothing but destruction in their wake.

Shuddering, Kulika sealed the book silently back in its drawer and continued her search, but there was little else of interest in the desk. Until she opened the very last drawer, and reached right to the back, where she found a deck of playing cards she recognised from the night before.

Jensen Mardh. Carolyn Villiers. Valencia Khan.

Photos, descriptions, last known whereabouts. With a sinking feeling in the pit of her stomach, Kulika realised that she was holding a missing persons deck in her hands. She flicked through it quickly, looking for a Jane, the name that had thrown Bartholomew so much when the kid had mentioned it to him last night. She didn't find one, but she did find that there was one card missing from the deck. Whoever this Jane was, Bartholomew had taken her picture from the stack, which only confirmed Kulika's suspicions: she meant something to him.

It wasn't much, but it was a start. And it was time to make herself scarce.

Putting everything back the way she'd found it, Kulika left the library and went searching for a way to get a message out to the baron. First, she looked for a phone, but apparently they were banned from the mansion, along with any other connection to the outside world. There was no hum of an internet router, no distant ringing, in fact nothing electronic at all beyond the lights. As far as Kulika could tell, the mansion had barely been upgraded since she'd been here last.

Next, she tested her exits: the road, the river, the woods. If she could get to Charleston, or even as far as a phone someone would let her borrow, then that would be enough. No such luck. It seemed that she could wander the property freely, but the moment she approached the boundary line, two or more Silver appeared and politely, but firmly, reminded her that Bartholomew would like her to remain at the mansion. She could fight her way out, in a pinch, but then she'd leave empty-handed.

In the end, she went back to the house. She didn't feel as though she had much choice.

It was still early enough that the heat of the day hadn't yet filled the inside of the house. In the breakfast room, the airy space that opened out onto the porch, the sun was slanting low through the closed glass doors. Kulika flicked the catch and slid them open, letting in the breeze.

She remembered the times when she would stand here alone in the dawn light, before. She'd done it often. The glass doors were new, but the porch had been here when she'd first arrived, three hundred years previously. She'd slept in the attic back then, in a box room that had been subdivided into little more than a cell that filled up with insects and wet heat in the summer. She'd wake before the rest of the mansion and come down here to sit out and enjoy the cool breeze coming off the river. Sometimes, she'd go to the water to fish or swim with Bayly, the mansion's only other early riser. They never talked, they just sat and existed in the freedom of the morning before Bartholomew woke and his covenant snapped back into place. It was the only time Kulika had ever felt free at the mansion, always with Bayly at her side.

'Morning.'

Kulika turned to see Bayly standing there, lounging against the wall on the other side of the doors, in the same place he had always stood. Something tight loosened in her chest, then. She'd been counting on his help in her search. To find herself abandoned last night, and to think herself abandoned again this morning… It had been a blow.

'You came back,' she said.

'I'm sorry I left,' he replied, his eyes fixed on the horizon, as always. 'I had business.'

'Bartholomew's business?'

'Who else's?'

Kulika stepped out onto the porch, and only then did the pool come into view, together with the detritus of last night's party. Whoever's job this was to clean up, they were clearly still asleep. There were empty bottles all over the grass, on the paving, even in the water, and smears of blood stained everything.

Too many humans around too many new Silver, all of them drinking. Of course it had ended badly.

'Is it like this every night?' she asked Bayly.

'Some nights,' he replied. 'Tuesdays get messier than most.'

Kulika leaned back against the porch railing and crossed her arms over her chest, waiting for Bayly to elaborate. When he didn't, she said, 'Don't you think it's time you told me what's going on here?'

'You know what's going on,' he replied.

Kulika had a terrible feeling that she did. She thought about the number of Silver she'd seen around the pool last night, the number of covenant tattoos on palms human and Silver, the number of signatures in the book, and the size of the new buildings that looked like nothing so much as barracks.

'He's preparing for war,' Kulika said.

Bayly didn't reply, but then, he didn't need to.

'Why the humans?' she asked.

Bayly shrugged. 'Every army needs a supply train.'

'And your involvement? I can't help but notice that you're not wearing the tattoo.'

Bayly looked at his boots, tapping one heel contemplatively against the opposite toe. It was clear from his body language that he wasn't going to tell her.

'That would be me,' said a voice from beyond the porch. The man came up the side of the house from the driveway. He was neat-looking, wide-shouldered, white, with sandy-blond hair, a square jaw, and bright blue eyes. 'Hi,' he said to Kulika, climbing the porch steps and offering her his hand, tattooed palm and all. 'I'm Enzo.' His accent was Italian, but his smile was all American: big, too-white teeth and oozing charm.

'Kulika,' she said, shaking his proffered hand. She was reluctant to touch the tattoo, but that was pure irrationality. There was no magic to it, she knew. She just hated the fucking things.

'I guessed who you were,' Enzo said, still smiling like a white-toothed shark. 'Bayly's told me a lot about you, though apparently he hasn't told you very much about me.' As he said this, he turned to Bayly with a wry smile. 'He's protective.'

'Uh-huh,' said Kulika.

Bayly said nothing at all.

'Well, I'm not here long,' said Enzo. 'Just dropping by to check in with Bartholomew, then I've got to get back to the lab.'

'Bella's still here,' said Bayly darkly.

'And I'll be gone before she sees me.' He turned to Kulika and explained, 'She used to be my assistant, at the lab.'

'What lab?' Kulika asked.

'BioSilver,' he said. 'I'm a research student there.'

'*BioSilver*?' Kulika repeated, but before she could ask anything else, Bartholomew called for Enzo from inside the house. For a second she wondered how he'd even known

Enzo was here, but if there were enough guards to chat with Kulika every time it looked like she might be leaving, there were surely enough to report on new arrivals.

'Got to go,' Enzo said, then he dropped a kiss on Bayly's cheek on his way into the house and was gone.

'He looks like a used car salesman,' Kulika said to Bayly once Enzo was out of earshot.

'I didn't ask for your opinion,' Bayly replied angrily.

'Well, you're getting it anyway. What kind of mess have you got yourself into? *BioSilver?*'

'It's the Primus's research lab.'

'I know what it is,' Kulika replied irritably. 'I work for Baron Drake, who works for the Primus, and I know what his fucking labs are called.'

'You asked,' Bayly harrumphed.

'No, I didn't. I was questioning whether you're *really* doing what I think you're doing, because if you were somehow involved in a plan to steal research or even Silver bioweapons from the Primus's lab, we both know that would be suicidally stupid.'

Bayly shrugged. 'If they want a war…'

Kulika gaped at him for a moment, not quite able to believe what she was hearing. 'Jesus Christ. When you asked if I was here to start a mutiny against the Primus, I didn't think you were serious.'

Solomon was technically only the Primus of the UK, but in reality he ruled a large chunk of the Silver population of the globe. The younger Silver outside of Britain didn't pay much attention to him, but that was only because they didn't know his history. If they had any idea of the carnage he'd wrought in his many millennia on the Earth, or how he'd clawed his way through blood and rebellion to position himself as the progenitor of the Silver in the first place, maybe they'd reconsider bending the knee. It was true that Baron Drake wasn't as deferential to the Primus as he might have been, but the baron was about as close to a peer as the Primus got these days. Even then, the current situation with Jack had raised tensions between the two right up to the breaking point.

If Kulika was going to stay loyal to the baron, she was resigned to the fact that she might have to defy the Primus one day. But preemptively sending spies into his facilities to steal his secrets? That was bold.

'Whose plan was it?' Kulika asked.

Bayly said nothing, he just turned his gaze back to his feet.

'Is Bartholomew making him do this?' Kulika pressed on. 'Or was this your idea?'

'I told him it was reckless,' Bayly said finally, clenching his jaw.

It was Enzo's plan, then. That made more sense. 'Trying to impress Bartholomew, was he? He must be new.'

Bayly didn't reply.

'You don't have to stay,' Kulika pointed out. '*You* haven't signed the Articles.'

'I sired him,' Bayly said.

'So? Bartholomew sired me. It doesn't mean anything.'

Bayly looked at Kulika sharply, dead in the eye.

Any human looking at him would have noticed nothing unusual, just as anyone looking carefully at Kulika or Bartholomew would have assumed they were nothing more than mortal. The silver tracery that patterned the whites of the eyes of the Silver was a signature they could learn to suppress, with focus and patience, and all the old pirates had been blessed with centuries in which to practice the skill. It was how they hid their existence from humanity, and it was yet another reason that Kulika was concerned that Bartholomew was turning so many new Silver at once. Either they were going to have to learn to hide their silver *extremely* quickly – even the luckiest among them would still take at least a few months, and some many years – or Bartholomew would have to keep all of them isolated on his property. Or, the third and most worrying option, perhaps he had no intention of keeping them hidden at all.

Then Bayly did something that was considered crass, or threatening, or even flirtatious amongst the Silver, depending on the context: he flashed his silver. Just for a second, he released the control that he held over the silver and allowed it to flood back into the tiny blood vessels in the whites of his eyes. It didn't stop there, though. Instead, it flooded into his irises, filtering through their natural brown colour like spokes before circling his pupil. Then the silver was all gone again, erased as Bayly exerted his control over it once more.

'Shit,' Kulika said.

Bayly had silvered for Enzo. That extension of the silver into the irises was something that happened when the Silver fell in love. It was the physical mark of Bayly's bond to Enzo, the same mark that Baron Drake had in his own eyes, representing his love for Jack. Bayly could no more abandon Enzo to Bartholomew than the baron could abandon Jack to burn to death from the poison in her veins. If Enzo died in this house, Bayly would die too. Their lives were tied together, forever.

'I feel like I should be giving you my condolences,' Kulika said. 'Could you not just take him and get out of here?'

'Because it was so easy to leave the first time,' Bayly scoffed.

'It's not going to get any easier, and if you're taking on

the Primus then you're all going to end up dead. You do realise that, don't you?'

'Things have changed since you left. Since we both left.'

'I can see that.'

'Well, you can't see everything.'

'I could help, Bayly,' Kulika said, exasperated. 'Maybe we could even help each other. I'm sure Bartholomew recognised Evita Khalyed from the picture, and I can tell you're holding back on me. So how about you give me some information to help me track down Dr Khalyed, then I get the two of us *and* Enzo out of here safely.'

'Right,' Bayly laughed dismissively. 'I can't help you, Kulika, any more than you can help me. You just look out for yours, and I'll look out for mine. All right?'

Then he walked away, down from the porch and around the side of the house to the driveway. A few minutes later, Enzo followed him out, waving to Kulika as he passed. She heard an engine start up on the other side of the property as he moved out of sight. It was a short visit for both of them, apparently.

She understood Bayly's reluctance, really she did. She wasn't unsympathetic. Leaving Bartholomew the first time had not been a simple matter. She wasn't sure how Bayly had done it, but back in the days before ubiquitous car ownership and women's rights, Kulika had needed to dress up in men's clothing just to get out of Charleston and onto a ship back home to England. Not that the concept of cross-dressing had been alien to her; it was how she'd become a pirate in the first place.

When Kulika had been young, the world had been different. Back then, you couldn't make your own way as a woman without earning it first. When Bartholomew and his pirates had boarded the *Onslow*, the ship that was supposed to be taking her across the Atlantic to her new husband, she'd seen it as an opportunity to rewrite her future. If she'd known just how dark that future would be, maybe she would have opted for the same route as her cousin Charlotte and just poisoned her husband instead. When Kulika counted up her sins under the black flag, she had to admit that a single straightforward murder would have been a quicker and less bloody path to independence.

But that wasn't the path she'd chosen. Instead, she'd disguised herself as a man before Bartholomew and his crew breached the cabin of the *Onslow*. She'd signed his Articles. She'd been tattooed with the mark of his covenant. Then she'd realised what he really was, and he'd made a different mark on her entirely. He must have known she was a woman all along, but he'd still broken his own rules to bring her onto the crew.

ARTICLE VI. No boy or woman to be allowed amongst them. If any man shall be found seducing any of the latter sex and carrying her to sea in disguise he shall suffer death.

Bartholomew hadn't died for breaking the terms of his own Articles. Escaping him, Kulika nearly had.

But she and Bayly were older now, stronger, cleverer. The world was different too, with fast transport and enough people to get lost in. Surely it wouldn't be so difficult to escape a second time, particularly since Enzo was the only one who'd actually sworn the oath. Bayly had to be exaggerating.

Kulika was turning this over in her mind, worrying at its edges, trying to see what she'd missed, when she noticed an unusual scent. She followed her nose to the edge of the porch, to the spot where she'd seen the sunset-haired woman with her friends the night before. There was blood on the paving slabs there, spilling from their edge into the grass.

She was pretty sure that the scent was coming from the blood, but she needed to get closer to be sure, so she hopped over the porch railing and landed in a crouch next to it, then took a sniff.

Sunshine and oranges. Rosewater and crushed ivy leaves. Blackberries in hedgerows on cold autumn mornings.

It was the richest scent Kulika had ever encountered, layered and complex and a little bit different every time she breathed it in. That wasn't a characteristic of Silver blood. Usually, the Silver had a distinct personal scent that was easily recognisable to anyone who knew them well. This was different: a kaleidoscope of the seasons filling her nostrils.

It could be a mixed drink, she supposed. Maybe there was the blood of several different humans in this single spill. One thing was certain, though: the intoxicating scent couldn't belong to the woman with the sunset hair, because she was Silver.

Irrelevant, Kulika told herself, unsure why the memory of that woman kept distracting her. Then she caught that shifting, seasonal scent on the breeze, pulling her in the direction of the trees beyond the pool.

She followed it.

10

IN THE BLOOD cellar, the day was heating up fast, and Quick's stomach was beginning to grumble. She should be packing up her hotel room now, getting ready to catch her plane this evening. It looked as though she was going to miss her flight, but right now that was the least of her worries.

'There'll be food soon,' Louis reassured her quietly.

She hadn't realised he was awake too. 'Sorry,' she whispered as her stomach grumbled again. 'Hope I didn't disturb you.'

'Nah. I woke up when Xiaoyu did.'

The lights were off, so there was only the faint glow from around the hatch to see by, but it was enough to illuminate Xiaoyu sitting alone on the floor between the sleeping area and the hatch.

'Didn't she take a watch shift?' Quick asked, thinking Xiaoyu would surely have needed a lie in to catch up.

'She did,' said Louis. 'Sometimes she doesn't sleep much, and then she gets like this.'

'Manic?'

'Let's say "vigilant".' Quick raised her eyebrows sceptically, and Louis added, 'Her instincts when she's like this are right more often than I can explain.'

As if to prove his point, there was a clunking noise from above, then the hatch was lifted clear.

'Breakfast!' a voice yelled. 'Get the fuck out the way, Xiaoyu.'

Then a man and a woman jumped down into the cellar. Vampires, Quick guessed; they treated the five-foot drop like it was an inch, barely even bending their knees to take the impact. The woman was blonde, busty and beautiful, and the man was the male version of her. They could have been twins, or Ken and Barbie, immortalised perfection. Seeing the two of them now, and thinking back to meeting Penny and Brandon last night at the party, Quick couldn't believe she hadn't picked up on the truth sooner.

'Who's doing the Casting this week?' Xiaoyu asked the man.

'Getting jealous, are we?' the woman replied.

'I didn't ask you,' Xiaoyu snapped at her. Then she turned back to the man to ask, 'How many?'

'Not you,' the woman said, 'that's all you need to know. And anyway, we've got a little surprise lined up for you before then.'

The man pulled paper bags down from the edge of the hatch, one after another, and slung them into the cellar as the woman walked over to the bathroom corner to collect a pile of full bin bags, three in each hand.

'Well?' Xiaoyu pressed.

'You'll find out soon enough,' the man replied.

The woman laughed on her way back to the hatch, saying, 'You tease.'

Then they jumped back out again, taking the bin bags with them, and shut the hatch behind them. Quick had the unsettling feeling that she was a hamster whose cage had just been cleaned out.

'Watch out for that one,' Xiaoyu said ominously as Quick and Louis joined her.

'The guy?' Quick asked.

'The woman. Bella, her name is.'

'Why?'

Xiaoyu sighed. 'Just watch out.'

The others were crowding close now, coming to collect their bags of food. Someone turned the lights on. There was no pushing, no fighting, no squabbling over who got what. When Quick opened her own bag, she understood why. Inside, the rations were basic: apples, bread, raw carrots, crackers. There was nothing here to fight over.

'Bella was down here for a while,' Louis said as he munched on a carrot.

'But she's a vampire,' said Quick.

'She is now, but back when I first got here, she was just one of us. She was nice, too. Scared, like all of us, but kind of sweet. A bit naïve, maybe.'

'But she lost it when they turned her?' Quick guessed. It made sense, because how else could you convince yourself to drink human blood when you'd so recently been a human yourself? The only way she could make it add up was if the transformation did something to the brain.

So she was surprised when Louis said, 'No. Not then. Thing is, she was head over heels for this guy, sure he was going to be rescuing her any second. She didn't realise he was the one who put her down here in the first place. Then after he turned her, they both disappeared for a while on some secret mission no one talks about, and she came back alone. She's been waiting for him ever since. *That's* what broke her.'

'She's got a broken head, not a broken heart,' Xiaoyu

scoffed.

'Maybe they're not all that different,' Louis replied.

'Whatever. I've had enough,' Xiaoyu said. 'Everyone's got a fucking love story, and it's boring as shit. I'm showering.'

Xiaoyu walked off to the bathroom corner, passing everyone else who'd gathered back in the sleeping area. Some were breaking open their bags, some weren't even bothering.

'Is it the same food every time?' Quick asked Louis.

'More or less. We only get the good stuff when we go upstairs to feed them. That's the carrot, you could say.' He huffed a bleak little laugh and took a bite of the literal carrot in his hand.

'How often does that happen?'

'The feeding? At first, a couple of times a week. After that, it takes longer to recover. Sometimes we get injections and stuff, but people get worn out after a while, and they bring in new people to replace them.'

'You mean they just kill us when we *wear out*?' Quick asked with horror.

Louis shrugged. 'Some of us they turn, like Bella, and we get to see those ones again. Most of them, though, they just don't come back.'

'Bloody hell.'

Some great detective Quick had turned out to be. She'd come to this place hoping to find Jensen, maybe even Evita, and now she was going to die here. Which made her wonder.

'Maybe my friend was here, once,' Quick said quietly. 'It was December when she went missing.'

'Maybe,' Louis replied, but he didn't sound convinced.

Quick didn't want to believe it either. If Evita had been turned into a vampire, she would have been at the party last night. If she had come to this place but remained human, she'd be in this room right now. The inescapable truth was that if Evita had indeed come this way – and Monty's reaction to her picture suggested she had – then she was dead.

But it would be an answer, at least, and the end to a six-month-long mystery that only Quick had cared enough to investigate. And look where that had got her. Quick would be the mystery, now. The difference was that no one would come looking for her.

Evita and Quick were both lonely souls. They'd found each other at university, bonding over the losses that had isolated them in the first place – abuse, random violence, illness – and the university itself had become a shared refuge. Not the university where they'd studied, because they'd outgrown that, but the institution of scholarship itself. With the bickering, the infighting, and the pettiness of intellectualism, the world of academia was like the dysfunctional family they'd never had, and they had it together. Their disciplines might not have been identical, but their shared sense of kinship was.

Then Evita had disappeared. Their colleagues had noticed she was missing, but only Quick had felt her absence like a wound. They would doubtless notice that Quick was missing now, and they'd wonder. Maybe they'd wonder enough to worry whether the same fate had befallen her as had caused Evita's disappearance, but they wouldn't worry enough to do anything about it. Maybe they'd comfort themselves by imagining that Quick had found Evita, that they'd rekindled their college romance – a brief liaison back when Quick was still realising she was bi and Evita was still realising she wasn't – and ridden off into the sunset together.

Maybe, if she worked hard at it, Quick could imagine a

happy ending for Evita too. If she worked even harder, she might be able to imagine a world in which Evita was found, alive and well, and came looking for *her*.

But in the reality of this hot, dank hole, that was a stretch.

'No one's looking for me,' Quick murmured into her paper bag.

'Nor me,' Louis said. 'None of the others, either. It's part of how they pick us.'

'They *picked* us?'

'The people no one would notice,' Louis said bitterly.

'People who'd stay at a party until two in the morning on a Tuesday night 'cause they got nowhere else to be, and no one waiting on them,' said a man who was chewing sadly on a slice of worthless white bread. 'None of us got no one.'

People around him murmured their agreement, then settled down quietly to their rations. They were all quiet. Over a hundred people in this cellar, and there was nothing but quiet compliance. That was strange, wasn't it?

Quick left her bag of food on the ground beside Louis and started walking around the room, feeling the walls, digging at the dirt in the corners, prodding at the ceiling in the places where it cracked.

'What are you doing?' asked Louis.

'Looking around,' Quick replied. Between the blood loss and the zombie, she hadn't taken the opportunity to scope it out last night, but now that the lights were on and she was starting to think clearly, she knew exactly what she had to do.

Scope out the terrain. Work out the best exit. Plan an escape. Even if it meant taking on the vampires and going out through the hatch, there had to be a way out of here, and Quick was going to find it.

A lot of hours later, Quick had a sore back, sore knees, dirt caked under her bloody fingernails, and a load of bug bites she'd rather not think about. She knew all too well that if she got bitten by some deadly American spider in this cellar, help would not be coming, but she'd kept searching nonetheless: pulling at the plumbing in the bathroom area, pushing at the hatch in the ceiling, digging a yard down into the dirt by the wall before she unexpectedly hit rock. She didn't know much about geology, but she knew from listening to Evita's research that Charleston was built on sand and clay. The rock only made sense when she cleared a little more dirt away and found that it was in fact part of a large stone slab. Whatever this building was, it had been built on the ruins of something else, ruins that she had no chance of shifting.

She yelled in frustration, then Xiaoyu threw a handful of dirt at her.

'Shut up,' she said. 'Don't attract attention.'

'So that's all you do all day?' Quick asked, brushing the dirt from her face as she looked from Xiaoyu to Louis, who was lounging next to her on the floor, then to all of the other cellar inhabitants who were dozing or talking quietly in their own little groups. 'You just sit around and wait for them to come for you?'

'Yep,' said Xiaoyu.

'And none of you are going to help me find a way out?'

'Nope.'

Quick yelled again. Xiaoyu threw more dirt. Most of it landed in Quick's hair and wouldn't shake out again.

'Stop it!' Quick yelled.

'You stop it,' Xiaoyu replied calmly.

'Look,' Louis said, 'everyone goes through this stage.'

'What?' Quick blinked the dirt out of her eyes.

'Idiot,' Xiaoyu said irritably. 'Do you think we've just been sitting down here for months with our thumbs up our asses? If there was a way out, we would have found it by now. We've all tried, and now we're all tired, and literally drained. There's no way out except through the hatch, which is locked tight from the other side. When it's opened, the vampires are there, and they kill anyone who tries to get out. No one is coming to save us. No one gives a shit. So sit down, shut up, and eat your damn carrots.'

Tired and out of options, Quick went and rinsed her hands under the tap, then did as Xiaoyu said.

'Feel better?' Louis asked as Quick bit into an apple.

'Not really.'

'Yeah. Well.'

'We're all going to die down here, aren't we?'

'Not necessarily,' Louis replied cautiously. 'Some of us'll go to the Casting on Friday, and who knows? We might get lucky and survive it.'

'Oh, right,' Quick said, recognising the word from Xiaoyu's conversation with the vampires. 'What is that?'

'The Casting?' Louis said. 'It's the ceremony where they try to turn people into vampires. Every Friday they do it, up at the house.'

'You've been?' Quick asked, curious.

'If I had, I'd either be a vampire or a zombie or dead.'

'And you call that *lucky*,' Xiaoyu chipped in sardonically.

'Sure, if you get turned,' said Louis. 'Better vampire out there than dead down here.'

'Is it? One way or the other, no one comes back from the Casting,' Xiaoyu said darkly, then she walked back towards the hatch, leaving Quick with Louis.

'Is she expecting something?' Quick asked.

'No,' Louis replied. 'The hatch won't open again until dinnertime, so you might as well rest while you can.'

Then the hatch cracked open, making a liar of him. It

panicked Xiaoyu. She was in her defensive stance between the hatch and the rest of the humans before the thing was even half-raised.

'Shit,' said a quiet voice from the floor above, then a face peeked into the gap left between the half-open hatch and the ceiling.

It was the woman Quick had seen last night at the party, the woman who walked like she was walking into battle. Her platinum-bleached hair fell over her eye as she peered down into the cellar and looked at them all one by one. Was it Quick's imagination, or did she hesitate for just a moment longer when she saw Quick's face?

'You're all human down here?' the woman asked.

'What's it to you?' Xiaoyu asked. 'Who are you?'

Not one of the vampires, then, Quick thought. Or perhaps she only hoped.

Praying she was right, she looked closely at the woman's eyes in the lights of the fluorescents, taking a few steps closer to make sure, until she was barely six feet away. By that point she was certain: there was no silver in her eyes. The woman who moved like a warrior was not a vampire. Perhaps she might yet prove to be Quick's salvation.

'I'm… I'm sorry,' the woman said. It felt for a moment as though she was speaking only to Quick, but then her gaze moved on to Xiaoyu and the others. Her accent was English, her voice iron-hard and rich. 'I can't get you out. Yet,' she added. 'They haven't gone far.'

'But you are *going* to get us out?' Xiaoyu asked.

The woman looked uncertain for a second. She said, 'I'll try,' then froze, listening. 'Got to go,' she said, and she closed the hatch again.

Quick looked around at the dirty, drawn faces in the cellar. They looked back, and at each other. No one seemed quite sure what to make of what had just happened.

'What was that?' someone asked.

'False hope,' Xiaoyu said with exhaustion in her voice. 'Go back to your nap.'

Some of them did, but despite her aching body and the energy drag she was starting to feel deep in her bones, Quick couldn't sleep. Unlike Xiaoyu, she still had hope.

11

MORE THAN A hundred humans in the cellar beneath the new block. Kulika had spent hours carefully searching the mansion and its surroundings before the newly-turned vampires had finally cleared out enough to give her a route into the building. Some kind of meeting at the house, it looked like. Kulika was torn, trying to decide whether her time would best be spent eavesdropping at the mansion or poking around in the new block, but the beguiling scent was still drawing her on, and it made the decision for her.

She found the cellar hatch in a double-locked cupboard hidden behind what looked for all the world like an ordinary wall. She wasn't sure what she'd been expecting to find beneath it – vanquished enemies, feral vampires, pirate treasure – but Bartholomew had sealed the cellar up tightly, with soundproofing and god knows what else, so Kulika had gone in practically blind. All she'd been able to tell was that there were things moving around beneath her. Then she'd seen far too much, too many starved bodies, and in the middle of them all: the sunset-haired woman.

Not Silver, after all. She was human, and captive. Bartholomew's captive.

Kulika knew from personal experience just how traumatic that could be, but she'd still walked away and left the woman in the cellar with the others. Now she was dealing with the aftermath of that decision.

More than a hundred humans Kulika had just abandoned to god-knew-what fate, all to preserve the faint hope that she might be able to save her baron and his reckless lover. The maths didn't add up, but it was what she had chosen. She consoled herself with the fact that it hadn't been much of a choice at all. If she'd tried to get the humans out, then the minute they'd got close to the boundary line, Bartholomew's goons would doubtless have jumped into action. Then Kulika would have lost any chance she had of getting the answers she needed, and the humans would have been herded back to the cellar, having gained nothing.

So many of them trapped down there, and for what? For food, for turning, or for fun? Bartholomew could be sadistic, but that many victims?

And she'd left them all to die.

Just like Bartholomew had done at Whydah.

The memories spun in her head, too similar for comfort.

The *Porcupine*.

It had been three centuries ago now, 1722. Just six months after she had been turned Silver, they had found the ship at anchor with ten others off the African coast of what was now Benin. Bartholomew had had only three ships of his own, one of which was just a supply ship, but they'd all arrived when the captains and traders were ashore conducting their business. Those left behind on the merchant ships surrendered readily enough to the pirates. Bartholomew sent a boat to shore with his ransom demands – gold dust for the safe release of the merchant ships at anchor – and ten of the captains agreed to his terms. The captain of the *Porcupine* did not.

In retaliation, and to prove that his threats were serious, Bartholomew set the ship alight.

The *Porcupine* was almost fully-loaded with a cargo of eighty enslaved Africans. Some jumped overboard in an attempt to escape, but they were chained in pairs, and there were sharks.

Despite all the lives he'd taken before that day, and all the terrible sins he'd committed since, it was the *Porcupine* that had finally broken Kulika's trust in Captain Bartholomew Roberts. But by then it had been too late: she had signed his Articles. She was his until he discarded her, or she would answer to the rest of the crew.

ARTICLE VII. He that shall desert the ship or his quarters in time of battle shall be punished by death or marooning.

Under Bartholomew's flag, they had always been in time of battle.

Judging by the shouts that were coming from the mansion when Kulika emerged from the block, not much had changed in the past century. She had thought it was odd when every Silver in the place headed up to the house together, giving her the run of the block. It was as if they'd been responding to some silent signal. Kulika hadn't heard anything, and she'd been listening, so she could only imagine that this was a congregation they'd been waiting for. Perhaps, she speculated, it had something to do with the phone call Bartholomew had taken this morning.

She followed the noise up the porch steps, through the breakfast room to the large open hall where the staircase swept gracefully down from the upper storeys. That was where she found the mob, crowded thick around the edges of the room and baying, like a pack of dogs held back only by the fear of their master. In the centre, lying at the bottom of the stairs, was a young, tattooed man with dark hair long enough to cover his face, but not the blood that pooled on the floorboards around it. Kulika had no doubt that Bartholomew was behind the beating, though she was just as certain that he hadn't personally laid a finger on him. That honour belonged to the young woman who was standing over him with a bloody knife in her hand.

Kulika could smell the blood. That wasn't unusual, but the way it clawed its way into her nostrils and thudded into her chest was. It was like inhaling a drug. That was the moment Kulika realised she'd allowed herself to become too thirsty, and too hungry. She was in no shape for a fight.

'This isn't your business, Kulika,' Bartholomew said from the first floor. He was standing at the mezzanine railing that overlooked the hall, gazing down at the carnage, pulling the strings of the Silver below like a puppeteer in his fly tower.

At his words, the crowd stilled.

Kulika stopped at the edge of the room and looked around. There were scores of Silver there, all apparently happy to participate in whatever this was. There hadn't been even a fraction of that number in residence in the days of Kulika's covenant to Bartholomew. She didn't recognise any of the congregation from back then, but she could pick out at least fifteen of them who were old enough to hide their Silver, and who were maybe even older than Kulika, judging by the sensitivity with which they reacted to their surroundings. Kulika had expected the newbies, but it was an unpleasant surprise to find this many experienced Silver allied with Bartholomew. Their presence wouldn't be enough to control the new ones, but it was definitely enough to start a war.

'Your crew's grown a bit,' Kulika said to Bartholomew, breaking the silence while the others warily watched her, watched the bloody scene at the foot of the stairs, and watched their glorious leader presiding over it all.

'You're naïve to think this is the full complement,' he replied. 'But this is their justice to exact, not yours.'

'Article seven?' she asked, stalling while she tried to work out how best to play the situation.

'You're not crew,' said the woman with the knife. It was dripping blood onto the back of the man's head, but he wasn't reacting to the sensation. From what Kulika could hear from her spot by the door, he wasn't even breathing. Whatever the woman had done to him with that blade, it was serious enough that he hadn't healed yet. Hearts could take hours to heal, brains sometimes a day, and that was if the Silver was older and stronger. If the guy on the floor was a new convert, it could take a week, if he ever woke up at all.

This is how Bartholomew enforced his power. He didn't get his hands dirty; he let other people dirty their hands for him. That was how he liked things. It was in all the books, that quote of his.

Since he had dipped his hands in muddy water, and must be a pyrate, it was better being a commander than a common man.

Kulika was certain he'd never said those words himself – he would never be so straightforwardly supercilious – but they were the kind of words other people could put in his mouth easily. They suited him well.

'You're not a part of this,' said the woman with the knife.

'Unless you want to be,' Bartholomew invited from the balcony above.

Kulika felt her lip curl involuntarily with disgust. 'I don't want any part of this.'

'He broke the covenant,' Bartholomew said, gesturing to the broken and bloody man on the floor. 'He was *disloyal*. You've done much worse than this to people much less deserving than him.'

She couldn't deny the accusation, because it was true. Back on the *Royal Fortune*, Bartholomew's flagship, she'd spilled enough blood to drown them all. Some of that bloodshed had been ordered by Bartholomew, but Kulika would be lying if she said that she hadn't wanted the carnage. Revelled in it, even. She'd learned the craft of death at Bartholomew's feet, and she'd learned it well enough to yearn for it when she was denied her fill. Perhaps she'd developed an appetite for it over time, or perhaps she'd simply recognised – as all the crew had eventually – that they could buy Bartholomew's favour with brutality.

'You used to understand what loyalty meant,' Bartholomew continued, turning his back on the mob to make his way down the stairs. 'Then the great Baron Drake came along, a guest in my house, and you stole away with him in the middle of the day, abandoning your captain and your crew.' He turned the corner of the staircase so he was walking towards them now, descending the stairs with the grace of a debutante at a cotillion. 'Back on ship, we used to have a word for that.'

'It's not mutiny if you've served out your commitment,' Kulika said.

'Oh, yes. Article nine. *No man shall talk of breaking up their way of living till each has a share of £1,000.*'

'I made you a thousand times that amount, at least.'

'But how much more did you owe me for what I made you?' Bartholomew asked. He was at the bottom of the stairs now, stepping carelessly over the unconscious man as though he were a sleeping dog, then crossing the floor to stand face to face with Kulika. 'Look at you,' he breathed, standing too close, so close that she could feel the heat of him. She wanted to step away, but that would be the worst kind of surrender in front of his followers, so she stood firm. 'Without me, you'd be three hundred years dead in childbirth for the whelps of some grey-bearded coloniser. With me, you are a finely-honed weapon of teeth and muscle and bone. Are you truly so ungrateful for what you've become?'

'I became what I had to in order to survive,' she said quietly. 'But you take more than you give.'

Bartholomew snatched her hand up in his own, turning her palm to the sky so he could trace its lines with his fingertips. He pressed his thumb gently to the spot where his black mark had once been inked and whispered, 'Only because you always discard what I give you. I'm offering you the whole world. We're taking it, Kulika, and I want you at my right hand when we do. Don't dismiss that without giving it some consideration.'

The words sounded as though he meant them, which threw Kulika. She'd expected threats, she'd expected recriminations, but she hadn't expected sincerity, nor had she expected such a bald statement of his intentions. She'd worked out that he was building an army, because that was hard to miss, and she'd guessed that he was going to force a revelation of the Silver to humanity, because that was exactly the kind of chaos on which Bartholomew had always thrived. What she hadn't anticipated was that he would have set his sights so wide. When he'd offered her the world, she hadn't taken it literally.

That had clearly been a mistake.

'Think on it,' he said. Then he stepped back and surveyed his followers with a smile, raising his voice to address them. 'In the meantime, we have business.'

The crew cheered.

'Read the charges, Bella,' said Bartholomew.

A curvy blonde, dressed for a ball in a floor-length red

satin gown, stepped forward and started reading, incongruously, from a couple of bright yellow sticky notes that had been stuck together. 'Alex – the accused of this crew – turned Leo Silver, but he didn't take responsibility for him in accordance with Article fifteen. Instead, he allowed him to leave the property in breach of Article fourteen, and Leo then used his Silver abilities off the property and in front of a human, in breach of Article twenty, all of this being done without the approval of the captain that's required by Article twelve.'

'Jessamy,' said Bartholomew. 'Your testimony.'

The woman with the knife turned to Bartholomew. 'It's like I told you, Captain,' she said, pushing her hair away from her eyes with the back of one bloody hand. 'I thought Alex got your permission to have Leo leave the property. I think Leo even thought he had permission, because me and Alex were supposed to go and drop off some bottles of blood with him this morning so he could stay home in Oklahoma a while. Then it looks like he was crushing on the girl next door, and he bit her, then tried to heal her and... Well, you've seen the bodies. You've seen the video, even.'

'And luckily for you,' Bartholomew said to her, 'I've seen you on the security video as well, so I know that you're telling the truth. Otherwise, I might find that story a little hard to believe.'

Jessamy visibly relaxed, her white-knuckled grip on the knife slackening as her shoulders fell.

'And the sentence?' Bartholomew asked, looking around the room now, his gaze touching briefly on the face of every single person gathered there.

All except Kulika. Bartholomew might be pretending that she wasn't in the room, but she suspected that, now that she was here, at least some of this performance was for her benefit.

Join us, or watch what'll happen if you don't.

'Death,' said an anonymous Silver in the crowd.

'Death,' said another.

Bartholomew smiled, and it wasn't long before the entire room was chanting the word, loud and demanding.

'As you've spoken,' he said, 'so it shall be, by the code. Jessamy, if you please.'

The woman with the knife grimaced momentarily before hiding her expression – not quickly enough – then crouched down with the knife in her hand beside the unconscious man. At least, Kulika hoped he was unconscious, given what happened next.

First, Jessamy rolled the man onto his back. Next, she pulled up his bloodied T-shirt to expose his naked stomach. Then, with the practised skill of someone who had done this before, she sliced into his abdomen, stuck her hand in up to the wrist, rooted around a bit, stuck the knife in again, and finally emerged with her bloody hands full of what Kulika judged to be about a third of his liver, which Jessamy brought over and presented to Bartholomew.

The others piled in on the body then, each drawing a knife from somewhere about their person or borrowing one from a friend. For a while, there was nothing but a huddle of people surrounding a nexus of wet, sawing sounds that Kulika wished she wasn't hearing. When they all pulled back and returned to their places at the edge of the room, each of the crew was holding a bloody mass in their hands and there was nothing left of the body but a smear of blood and hair on the floor.

'What now?' Kulika asked Bartholomew, covering her nausea with bravado. It turned out that, after a hundred years away, she was no longer hardened to such bloodthirstiness.

'You feed him to the alligators?'

'Not the gators, no,' he said. 'We're more frugal than that. Waste not, want not. Blood is blood, after all.'

With a savage smile, he raised the dripping fistful of liver to his mouth. Then, with his eyes locked on Kulika's, he bit down. Apparently this was the cue that the rest of them had been waiting for, because now they raised their own excised pounds of flesh to their mouths, with varying degrees of relish. But still, whether they held muscle or sinew, organ or bone, they followed Bartholomew's lead without question.

Piece by bloody piece, they ate him.

12

THE NEXT MORNING, Kulika was still at the mansion, though not by choice. She'd tried to make an exit after seeing Bartholomew's new cult in action, but then he'd said, 'Stay another night,' and the scores of cannibalistic, blood-smeared Silver who now comprised his crew had taken that as an order. She hadn't been offered the opportunity to refuse.

It wasn't until she woke that she discovered that not only was her suite in the mansion right next to Bartholomew's, but the two shared a connecting door. She'd flopped straight into the grand four-poster bed without washing or changing her clothes, not because she was still keeping vigil – though she probably should have been – but because she couldn't find the duffel bag she'd brought with her. When she went looking for it that morning in what she'd thought was a cupboard, she found something worse.

The door didn't lock from Kulika's side.

'Good morning,' Bartholomew greeted her as he pulled the inner door to his suite open. His, Kulika noticed, was fitted with a lock and key. 'Did you sleep well?'

'I did,' she said with irritation, 'but only because I didn't know about this door.'

He laughed dismissively. 'You'll feel better when you've eaten. Come down to the dining room and grab something from the buffet.'

'You lay on a buffet breakfast, now?' When she'd lived here a century ago, in much more modest quarters, it had been all porridge and rice and help yourself to a ladleful from the pot on the fire, and count yourself lucky if you get there before it's all gone. Yesterday, she'd eaten only a cereal bar from her jacket pocket for breakfast, then a sandwich that she'd scrounged from the kitchen of the new building for lunch, and nothing for dinner. After the theatrical demise of Alex, she'd found she'd rather lost her appetite. This morning, it had come back with a vengeance.

'You might have noticed that there are more of us to cater for nowadays,' Bartholomew said.

'I wouldn't have thought they'd be hungry after yesterday, after all that protein,' Kulika replied darkly, her stomach churning again at the memory.

'Oh, don't be like that,' he laughed. How was he *still* laughing, after everything she'd seen?

'I came here for information about Evita Khalyed,' she said. 'I don't know what you were trying to prove with that display last night—'

'So sanctimonious,' Bartholomew laughed again. 'As though meting out justice isn't your entire purpose. I've heard the whispers coming out of the old country about what happens to Drake's prisoners. Those captives in his basement, the ones that are supposed to be under his protection during their sentences, how many of them live long enough to serve out their terms? He's nothing more than a rogue executioner, and you're his enabler.'

'The people he punishes are serial killers,' Kulika said, in a more defensive tone than the one she had been aiming for. It made her sound weak, and weakness wasn't something she ever wanted to show to Bartholomew.

'Silver serial killers, who've openly killed humans, yes?'

'Yes.'

'But that's not their *crime* in the eyes of the Primus and your baron, is it? Their crime is that by openly killing humans, they've risked revealing the existence of the Silver to humanity. What they really are is oath-breakers. So my question is: how are their crimes any different from the breaches of the Articles that Alex committed? Didn't he deserve his punishment more, not less, than the edict-breakers that your Drake murders cold-heartedly in their prisons beneath his mansion?'

'What the Primus and the baron consider their crimes aren't necessarily the same,' Kulika said, too defensively again.

'Different means, same ends?' Bartholomew asked.

'It's too early for sophisms,' Kulika replied irritably.

This was the problem with Bartholomew: he'd knot you up in your own arguments until you found yourself agreeing with him by accident. Then he had you trapped.

He laughed. *Again*. 'The point is that you've done worse to crew members who've done less, if not under Drake's orders then under mine.'

'But I'm not your enforcer anymore.'

'Just answer me this,' he insisted. 'How is what happened last night any different to the deaths you dealt to mutineers back on ship?'

'We didn't use to eat them!' Kulika yelled.

'Then we were wasteful,' he replied lightly, as though that were the end of the discussion. Kulika was left with the uneasy feeling she always had at the end of a debate with

Bartholomew: he'd won, and she'd lost, but she wasn't sure how or what. 'Come and have breakfast,' he said, heading past her to her bedroom door, then out into the corridor. 'No hunks of dead meat, I promise.'

She couldn't believe he was joking about it. No, actually, she could believe it. It just chilled her blood.

'You've forgotten who you are,' he said, then he turned his back to her and started walking down the stairs.

'No, I'd forgotten who *you* are,' Kulika said quietly. She'd been so focused on not becoming trapped here again, bound by Bartholomew's covenant, that she'd forgotten about the slow creep of immorality that infected everyone in close proximity to him. She'd forgotten how thoroughly you could lose yourself in the example of the people around you, and end up unconsciously following their lead. When the person leading was Bartholomew, that influence was beyond dangerous. As last night had demonstrated all too clearly, it could be fatal.

If Kulika could have picked up Evita Khalyed's trail from anyone else, then she would have done. As it was, she had no other options, so she followed Bartholomew down to the ground floor, intent on making him surrender the information she needed, and hoping desperately that she wouldn't have to follow him any further than that.

There didn't seem to be anyone else around in the mansion, but then it was late, the heat of the day already pervading the mansion. Anyone sensible, who hadn't been sleeping off days of overexertion and undernourishment, would have taken their breakfast hours earlier.

'I don't know why you're keeping me here,' Kulika said, close on Bartholomew's heels, 'but if you think that what you did last night is going to make me stay, then you're wrong.'

'Am I though?' he said, stopping at the foot of the stairs and turning to meet her as she reached the bottom step. 'Don't you remember what it was like on the ship? The fire, the fury, the blood. You loved it, Kulika. You can't pretend that you didn't. You know what it's like to yield to your soul's call to savagery, and you know the acceptance you can find from being around other people who hear it too. Or have you forgotten that I was there when you came into your strength?'

It was a day that Kulika had tried very hard to forget. Sometimes – not always, but sometimes – newly-turned Silver could go a bit... wrong. Most of them, if cared for properly, and if attentively fed with blood by their makers, could transition to life as one of the Silver with minimal danger to themselves or others around them.

Bartholomew had been neither proper nor attentive. That wasn't the way he'd run his ship.

When Kulika had wakened from Bartholomew's draining bite and found herself ravenous for blood in the middle of a boarding action in the waters off Sierra Leone, the crew of the prize hadn't stood a chance. She'd blazed through them like a hurricane, a mindless creature using powers she hadn't realised she'd had without any thought at all, driven only by her thirst. Bartholomew liked to say that the crew hadn't even had time to surrender, but Kulika knew that wasn't true. She remembered their pleas. She hadn't heard them in the moment, but they'd come back to her later, and every night since when she closed her eyes and tried to sleep. She knew full well that she'd killed unarmed men who'd offered her no resistance at all.

'And that was just the beginning,' Bartholomew whispered, leaning close. 'You forget how well I know you, and how well I know your vices. All I want to do is let you fulfil your darkest desires.'

'Why, Bartholomew?' she asked. 'Why do you even care?'

'I made you,' he said. 'You were mine. I lost you, and I have lost too much in recent months. Then here you are, falling into my lap again like a gift in the hour of my greatest need.' He reached out to cup her jaw with his hand, caressing her cheek with his thumb like a mother would her child's. His eyes were drinking in every inch of her, shining with hungry pride. 'I would have you back at my side,' he whispered. 'I see your reluctance, but you don't see my determination. You will be mine again, Kulika, not because I'll force it on you, but because you know that only I have the power to give you everything you want.'

'And if what I want is freedom?' she asked, stepping away and out of his reach.

'Do you have freedom now?' Bartholomew asked derisively. 'You haven't broken free, Kulika, you've just traded one captain for another. You'll have a better life on my crew than on his.'

'I like my life fine the way it is.'

'And when the Revelation comes?' Bartholomew asked softly. The bottom dropped out of Kulika's stomach. 'You know it won't be long now. We're prepared. Drake is not.'

'You're not prepared,' Kulika spat. 'You've just filled your mansion with untested new Silver who can't control themselves.'

'But they do, and they will, or they'll answer to me. They bear my covenant. They know what that means; you saw it yesterday. They're loyal.'

'I have my own loyalties,' Kulika said.

'And when the Silver are known to the world, how is an alliance with a washed-up baron who's defied his king going to protect you? The Primus will kill him, along with everyone who follows him, including you. You know this as well as I do.'

'Baron Drake has never defied the Primus.'

'Now you're lying to me?' Bartholomew said with disappointment. 'I can always tell when you're lying, Kulika.'

She looked at Bartholomew, at the intensity of his gaze and the determined set of his jaw, and she knew that her own matched his. He was as determined to keep her here as she was to leave.

'I'm going back to Baron Drake,' she said.

'He called this morning,' Bartholomew replied casually.

Kulika's stomach twisted. The baron had probably been trying to get hold of her, but of course he couldn't, because Bartholomew was holding her phone hostage. Probably for the best, because what would she have told him? That she was going to let both him and his lover die because she couldn't bear to be back under Bartholomew's thumb again? Now that she imagined relaying that to Baron Drake, it sounded terribly selfish. She was his head of security. It was her job to give her life to protect his. She had a duty to him, and she was failing it.

'We came to an arrangement,' Bartholomew said.

Kulika was surprised, perhaps even a little scared by that. Bartholomew might have been happy to barter with the lives of his crew, but that had never been the baron's style. He understood the value of autonomy. At least, Kulika had thought he did.

'What kind of an arrangement?' she asked.

'If you stay until Monday, I'll tell you everything I know about Evita Khalyed. Otherwise…'

Otherwise, she knew, she would get nothing at all.

It was Thursday. She could manage four more days for the sake of the baron's life, couldn't she?

'And what do I have to do during those four days?' Kulika asked suspiciously. 'What do I have to sign?'

'Nothing at all,' Bartholomew said, walking to the breakfast room doors on the other side of the hall. To get there, he crossed the bloodstained spot on the floorboards from the night before – one of many, Kulika saw. He flung the doors open and said, 'Just enjoy my hospitality for a few days. That's all.'

She hadn't agreed to Bartholomew's deal, not in so many words, but – tentatively – Kulika followed him.

In the breakfast room, the glass doors that opened out onto the porch were shut now, keeping out the heat of the day. Fans spun lazily from the ceiling, but there was no air conditioning to cool the breeze, and the old house was hot.

'Help yourself from the buffet,' Bartholomew said, sweeping an arm towards the wall to their left. On one side of the space, a table was stacked high with pastries, cut fruit and bread. On the other, a line of a dozen humans was being arrayed against the wall by a few of the young Silver. The humans all had their hands behind their backs. It took a moment for Kulika to spot the restraints bolted into the wall and understand their purpose.

'This isn't how we do things,' she said, backing away.

'Isn't it?' Bartholomew asked blithely. 'Well, with so many mouths to feed, it's how *we* do things.'

'Then you can do them without me,' Kulika said, walking clear through the room and out through the porch to the pool. Maybe a few laps would clear her head.

'You can't hold out forever,' Bartholomew called after her.

But that was where he was wrong. Since she'd left the mansion, Kulika had taught herself the one thing that was beyond Bartholomew's understanding: self-discipline. She could keep her appetites in check, and until she could find a more ethical blood source, that was exactly what she would do.

13

IN THE BLOOD cellar, time passed slowly, and Quick was growing impatient.

The bags of food kept coming, filled with the same fare every time. Quick kept looking for exit routes, but finding none. No one wanted to talk to her, too conscious of lost friends to risk making any more.

No one except Louis.

To pass the time during the long, empty hours, he lay next to her and whispered outrageous stories about his huge family, spread all across the South. Quick was sure they were more fiction than fact, and maybe that was why she liked them; the truth felt too bleak in this hole in the ground. In return, Quick told Louis how she'd met Evita, and recounted all the escapades they'd had travelling around the world together. Eventually, though, even those stories became infected with the knowledge that Evita had likely died in this place, and that the same fate would claim Quick before too long. When that reality struck her, Louis just slung an arm around her shoulders and pretended he didn't notice that she was crying.

Then the vampires came for him, and eleven others. At

first, Quick thought maybe Louis had got his wish, and they were taking him to the Casting, but that wasn't it. That wouldn't happen until tomorrow, he said. They needed blood, they said. There was a system, he said, and it was his turn, so he let them take him up through the hatch.

An hour later, the others came back.

Louis never did.

After that, Quick didn't make any more friends.

The blood cellar was disturbed on Thursday evening by the screaming thuds of a hell of a lot more people being flung down through the hatch. It was early enough in the evening that Quick had not yet managed to fall asleep, though that probably had less to do with the hour and more to do with the fact that she was lying on dirt in a stifling hot basement with a hundred other people, at least half of whom snored or screamed in their sleep.

When the proper screaming started, Quick sat bolt upright and prepared to run towards the blanket line – though god knew that wouldn't be enough to catch so many zombies – but Xiaoyu grabbed her arm and pulled her back to her sleeping spot.

'It's the Casting tomorrow,' she said. 'All of them are human.'

'So many, though?'

'There are always a lot on Thursdays,' said Xiaoyu, but she looked increasingly worried as more and more people were pushed into the cellar, wearing flimsy outfits or underwear or, in some cases, nothing at all. 'They have the big party in the middle of the week, then they sleep it off with the humans in their rooms, party some more on Thursday, then they need somewhere to put them all to cool down before Friday.'

'That happened to you?' Quick asked.

'To most of us,' she said, which didn't really answer the question.

The newcomers were being tossed in on top of each other now, some rolling across the dirt floor to thud against the walls, some trying to push their way back up through the hatch, but most of them just trying not to get crushed in the wide heap that was forming under the hatch.

'Not this many, though,' said Xiaoyu as she stood from her watch. 'Something's up.'

Without discussing it further, the existing cellar-dwellers got to their feet and shifted into a line that cut the cellar in two, with the bathroom area and bedding behind them, and the newcomers in front.

For the next little while, they did nothing but watch. The fluorescents had been off when the hatch opened, and the newcomers were making enough of a racket to mask any sounds of movement from the far end of the cellar, so they hadn't noticed that there were people already in residence. All of their attention was focused on the hatch as more and more people poured down on top of them. It took maybe ten minutes of solid, frenzied activity before the people who were inclined to try and fight their way out off the hatch had been subdued, and the rest had realised there was no point in following their lead.

There was a whole crowd of new additions by the time they were done. It was just as well that Quick had sworn off making new friends, because none of them looked like they would welcome it.

The hatch slammed shut, plunging them all into darkness. After a few seconds, someone in the far end of the cellar flicked the light switch on.

One of the newcomers, a college-age man who looked like he spent too much time in the gym, said, 'Who the fuck are you?'

One of the existing cellar residents squared up to him and said, unhelpfully, 'Who the fuck are *you*?'

Then the fighting started. Xiaoyu ended it with a whistle that was loud enough in the echoing space to have everyone covering their ears.

'Knock it off!' she yelled. 'Food's there,' she said, pointing at the stack of paper bags in the centre of the cellar. 'Bathroom's there.' She pointed to the corner. 'Welcome to the blood bank. Now settle the fuck down.'

And that, more or less, was the end of that. There were other questions – how do we get out of here (you don't), are we going to die (almost certainly), and who put you in charge (don't fucking start with me) – but soon enough, the newcomers stopped fighting.

As Quick had learned, there was no point.

14

KULIKA SPENT THE rest of Thursday in frustrating inaction. She couldn't get back into the block, because it was full of new Silver. She couldn't leave the premises, because Bartholomew's guards were on high alert. And she couldn't get information from any of the Silver about even the most innocuous thing, let alone the identity of the mysterious *Jane* whose card was apparently missing from the deck in Bartholomew's desk, because each and every one of them ignored her when she tried to talk to them. It was becoming clear that an order had been issued by their captain, and the crew was determined to obey it.

Having run out of other options, she even tried speaking to Bartholomew himself, *voluntarily*, but he was locked up in the mansion's wine cellar again on some secret business that Kulika couldn't get even a sniff of, however hard she'd tried, both metaphorically and literally. Her sense of smell was pretty good for a Silver her age, but she still couldn't pick up on any unexpected scents in the mansion, in its kitchen, or around the door to the wine cellar.

Feeling frustrated, and more than a little thirsty for the blood she was trying to pretend she didn't need, she grabbed a can of beer from the unnecessarily extravagant bar in the back garden and cracked it open on the porch.

It helped her to be somewhere familiar, however much the view had changed. Out here, in the place she had often retreated to think during the bad old days, maybe she could come up with a plan.

'Heard you've been asking around about Jane,' said Bayly, surveying her as he came out of the house to join her on the porch.

'How long have you been here?' she asked. She'd been searching for him all day with no luck, and she hadn't heard a car pull up.

'Stayed over last night,' he said. 'Got a room upstairs, same as you. Not as grand, of course.'

'You could have come to find me earlier.'

'No,' Bayly said quietly, looking down at where his elbows rested on the porch railing. 'I couldn't.'

Which was as good as saying that Bartholomew wouldn't have let him.

Kulika asked, 'Do you know who this Jane is that Bartholomew's being so secretive about?'

'Nope,' Bayly replied.

'Are you saying that because Bartholomew told you to?'

Bayly just shrugged.

'We didn't use to lie to each other, Bayly.'

'We used to be on the same crew,' he pointed out.

Which meant Kulika would get no more from Bayly than she had from any of the other Silver on the property. That was irritating, but not unexpected. After all, he had Enzo to think of.

There was noise coming from the mansion behind them now, voices calling to each other and music cranking up in the anticipation of some kind of party. They seemed to happen most days here.

'You were here last night, then,' Kulika said. 'For the... whatever that was.'

She hadn't seen Bayly in the cannibalistic crowd, but she'd felt him there. She'd hoped she was wrong, that Bartholomew wouldn't have been able to induce Bayly to take part, but she knew their erstwhile captain wouldn't have accepted anything less. One way or another, he made his followers follow him.

'That Silver, he was just a kid,' said Kulika.

'They're all kids, the new ones,' Bayly said. 'Alex was stupid.'

'Explain.'

Bayly sighed, and the sound was heavy. 'Kid's a barman in town. He turned this other kid called Leo, just a teenager. Too young for all this.' He waved a hand over his shoulder at the mansion, but it was unnecessary. Kulika knew what *all this* was. She'd been barely out of her teens when she'd lived it for herself, and still she hadn't lived long enough to enter Bartholomew's world. She wasn't sure that anyone could. 'And Leo was in love,' Bayly added.

'Silvered?' Kulika asked.

'The minute he went home to see his girl,' Bayly confirmed. 'So now Bartholomew's got a fresh Silver out of the mansion without his leave, still so new he has to wear sunglasses to hide his eyes, and Leo loses control. Bites the girl, drains her, tries to heal her and fails. She dies. He dies, killed by the bond to his love, so *now* Bartholomew's got two bodies, one of them Silver and the other human with a silver palm print on her skin, from where the kid tried to heal her through the bond.'

'Oh, god,' Kulika interjected. 'Is that why he's down in the wine cellar?'

Bayly tapped his nose, which as good as confirmed it.

'And, to top it all,' he went on, 'he's got surveillance video from the house, inside and out. The kid moving at Silver speed outside when he snatches the girl, the two of them inside the house, him biting her and trying to heal her. The whole thing. *Assets*, he says, but he's pissed off about it all the same, and someone has to pay for it, to keep order. With Leo dead, Alex gets the blame for letting him off the property, as if we don't bend that rule all the time. So here we are.'

For a man of so few words, it was a long speech, rapidly spoken. That was just one indicator to Kulika that Bayly was more than a little upset about it.

'You knew the kid?' she asked.

'I knew Alex. They're shits, these new ones. All of them, running around poking their sunglasses where they don't belong. But, just marginally, Alex was less of a shit than the others.'

'You ate him,' said Kulika. 'Part of him, anyway.'

Bayly's face shuttered. 'It's so they can't come back from it,' he said with a shrug.

'He wasn't coming back anyway, Bayly. We both know that. And even if he did happen to be some miraculously regenerative youngster, there's no reason *you* had to be the ones to eat him. You said they feed the mistakes to the alligators.'

'He says eating them makes us stronger.'

'What it's making you all is *insane*.'

'He says the power is in the blood, and consuming our dead keeps the power in the crew.'

'Of course he does,' Kulika said, throwing up her hands. 'He's just building a new vampire mythology on land to replace the pirate mythology he had on the water. You do realise that, don't you?'

'I'm older than you, Kulika,' Bayly said gruffly. 'I'm not part of the sunglasses brigade.'

It was true that Bayly's transformation pre-dated Kulika's own – he'd actually been there when the old pirate capital of Port Royal sank in the earthquake of 1692 – but apparently wisdom and age weren't that closely linked, because he was being an idiot.

'Get out of here,' Kulika said quietly. 'If you can see what he's doing so clearly, then just go.'

'And have them do to me or Enzo what they just did to Alex?' Bayly said incredulously. 'Bartholomew has them all believing that if one of us leaves without being consumed, it'll diminish our power. And he has trackers, good enough to find us anywhere in the world and bring us back to him. You saw them in there yesterday.'

'I saw some older Silver, but I didn't recognise them.'

'You wouldn't. A couple of them came up in the Gold Rush and stayed out west until Bartholomew started calling people this way. The rest came over from Japan and Russia, or down from Canada.'

'But why?' Kulika couldn't understand why so many ancient vampires would be flocking to join Bartholomew. 'It's not as though he's got anything special to offer.'

'Hasn't he?' Bayly asked.

'Has he?' Kulika asked.

But Bayly didn't answer. He just said, '*You* should get out of here, though.'

'Not without finding Evita Khalyed.'

'The longer you stay here, the harder he'll make it for you to leave.'

'I'm here until Monday, and that's it.'

'He's holding out on you until then?' Bayly asked.

'Yes,' Kulika admitted.

'It's not in your nature to sit and wait.'

'It's not in your nature to *eat people*, Bayly. I'm just doing the same as you: what I have to.'

'No, you're giving him time to change your mind,' Bayly said irritably. 'Just go. While you still can.'

'If I didn't know any better, I'd think you were trying to get rid of me.'

Kulika had been joking when the words left her mouth, but they landed in a way she hadn't expected. Bayly's lips twitched, then he looked down at the porch railing as though he were hiding his face.

'What aren't you telling me?' she asked.

'Nothing,' he replied defensively. 'Nothing you don't know. It's just… This is the line, Kulika. If you stay for tomorrow night…'

'Why? What's so special about tomorrow?' Bartholomew had been doing weekly Castings, she knew. She'd picked up that much from the chatter around the mansion. As rare as Castings were on her side of the world, they seemed almost run-of-the-mill here, so that couldn't be it.

'Everyone's here,' Bayly said, lowering his voice to a whisper. 'Everyone who has humans to bring is bringing them now, either to turn or to add to the blood bank, and Bartholomew's sworn humans are going the same way. He's tying up loose ends, then the rest of the crew is coming this weekend after… Look, that's what this is all about,' he said urgently. 'It's happening, and it's happening now.'

'What is?'

'He's got *assets*. The recordings.'

'What are you talking about?' Kulika asked, not following his train of thought at all.

'We're coming out. *Now*.'

A heavy weight settled in the pit of Kulika's stomach as she finally caught on.

They'd been fighting this battle in the UK for years now, half of the Silver wanting to reveal themselves to humanity and take charge, and the other half wanting to stay in the dark, where they felt safer. Over there, the Primus had always won out and kept them hidden, but if Bartholomew forced the point here in the States, the rest of the world wouldn't have much choice but to follow.

Wasn't that what Bartholomew had always wanted? More Silver followers.

If Bayly was right, he was about to have all the followers in the world.

15

NO ONE IN the blood bank slept well that night, which is to say that they slept even worse than they usually did. With the influx of new people, the atmosphere was restless. They were fighting over blankets, and food, and the crying and screaming just seemed to get louder and louder as the night went on.

When the hatch was flung open on Friday morning, Quick felt like she'd barely slept at all, but neither the newcomers' sleepless night nor their injuries were slowing them down. They crowded under the opening, clawing for it and shouting to be let out, as though the night had never intervened between their arrival and now.

'Quiet!' someone yelled from above the hatch. The voice sounded depressingly familiar. 'We need bodies. Where's Xiaoyu?'

In the spot beside Quick, Xiaoyu went very still. She'd taken Louis's place beside Quick without either of them discussing it, but that meant she'd had to abandon her watch of the hatch. She clearly hadn't been expecting it to open so soon.

'Back!' the guy yelled from upstairs. 'Move away from

the hatch or I'll break bones when I push you. Got it?'

The newcomers backed away slowly. They were shortly replaced by a single familiar vampire jumping down into the space, his gaze roaming through the darkness until it landed on Xiaoyu.

It was Monty.

'Shit,' Xiaoyu murmured, then she got quickly to her feet and asked, 'How many?' walking towards Monty as though by doing so she could shield the others in the cellar from his scrutiny.

'Twelve, for starters,' Monty said. 'Full house today.'

'Are they here for the Casting?' she asked.

'Sort of. Look, less questions, more volunteering. The redhead from the other night,' Monty said. 'She needs to go up.'

Quick's blood ran cold. He was talking about her.

'You already fed from her,' said Xiaoyu.

'She still needs to go, her and anyone else new this week who hasn't gone up yet. Make up the numbers with whoever. You pick them. None of last night's lot, though, not yet.'

Xiaoyu turned and walked back towards Quick, grim-faced. 'Sorry, Red,' she said quietly.

'He's going to bite me again, isn't he?' she asked, her hand flying to the still-raw wound at her throat.

'Probably not him, but one of them will. Nothing I can do except come along for the ride.'

It didn't take long for Xiaoyu to find enough people to make up the full dozen Monty demanded, picking those who were most able to spare the blood. By the time they made their way to the hatch, two vampires Quick didn't recognise were in the hole keeping the newcomers back, while another stood under the hatch ready to help Quick and the others up. Monty had disappeared.

'It's not so bad,' Xiaoyu said reassuringly – which would have been more convincing if Quick wasn't still sore from the first bite – then the vampire hoisted her out of the hatch. The others followed, leaving Quick until last.

Upstairs, it was quiet. Maybe the other vampires were sleeping it off, or maybe they weren't home. Either way, there were just the three of them there to corral Quick and her cellar-mates through the communal showers on the ground floor – there was no regard for modesty in the blood bank – then into the walk-through wardrobe next door. The clothes were mismatched and worn, chucked in disordered piles, but they were at least clean, and after a little sifting Quick found a loose cotton dress in a size that would fit her. There were no shoes.

When they emerged from the building, blinking in the morning sunshine, the grass was dry and prickly under Quick's bare feet. It had to be mid-morning, judging by the angle of the sun, and it was already hotter than Quick could bear. More than a couple of minutes out in this and her skin would be lobster red.

'Hurry it up,' said one of the vampires in the back, then Monty reappeared from around the side of the building and took Quick's upper arm in a firm grip.

'Look, Quick,' he said in a hushed voice. 'I'm sorry about —'

'*Sorry*?' Quick replied incredulously, twisting as he marched her across the lawn so she could look him in the face. 'What for, Monty? For biting me? For lying to me? Or for throwing me in a cellar with a hundred other people so you and your friends can slowly drain me to death?'

He changed, then. He was one of those men, at his core. Before she'd snapped back, he'd been all apologies and reconciliation, but the moment he saw she wasn't going to buy it, he brought out his teeth.

'I am more dangerous than you can possibly imagine,' he said softly. His words carried all the more threat for the gentleness with which they were delivered, but Quick was tired and sore and she'd been pushed to her limit.

'If you're going to kill me,' she said, 'then do me a favour and kill me quick.'

'I probably will tonight,' he said irritably. 'You're going to the Casting.'

If Monty hadn't been holding Quick up, she would have fallen.

'I'm what?' she asked.

'You're going to the Casting,' Monty repeated.

Nausea tugged at the back of Quick's throat. She remembered everything Louis and Xiaoyu had told her about her chances of turning vampire or zombie, and suddenly being slowly bled to death over a period of weeks didn't seem like such a bad way to go. At least it meant she wouldn't have to die tonight.

'I'm sorry, Quick,' Monty said, 'but you haven't given me much of a choice.'

'Really?' she said incredulously. 'So when you lied and told me Jensen Mardh had been here, that you could help me find him, that wasn't a choice? Because I was ready to leave that bar and get right on my plane back to the UK until you *chose* to tell me that.'

'Jensen was here,' Monty said. 'I didn't lie about that.'

'What?'

'We tried to turn him. It didn't work.'

'You mean he turned into a zombie?'

'Don't use that word,' he said, shushing her as he looked around at the others to check if they'd heard. From the pissed-off looks on their faces, Quick guessed they had. 'I mean he's *gone*, like a lot of the people in your little pack of cards.'

'And Evita?' Quick whispered, tears pooling in her eyes. She'd known her friend was most likely dead, and had almost resigned herself to it, but now that she was having it confirmed—

'*Don't* say that name,' Monty said under his breath. 'Ever. I mean it. It'll get you killed here.'

'If I'm dying tonight anyway, then what does it matter?'

They'd reached the house now, but Monty pulled Quick to a stop as the others filed inside.

'I'll be there in a minute,' he told them, then he pushed her back up against the porch railings and held her there, pinning her upper arms with his hands.

'Look, Quick,' he said. 'I know this hasn't exactly gone to plan, but the boss says either you're going to the Casting tonight or you're dead. I'm trying to save you here, but I need a little cooperation. The others who are up for the Casting, they've had time with the people who're sponsoring them. They've built some kind of relationship, at least. But we don't have that, and without it I won't be able to turn you Silver. So either you get stubborn about it and die, or you try to find some kind of positive feeling for me so you at least have a chance of living through the Casting, because that's what it takes.'

'What are you talking about?' she said.

'I know you've seen what happens when we try to turn someone Silver and it goes wrong. You just said it.'

With a grimace, Quick remembered the zombie in the cellar.

'Yeah, well,' Monty continued. 'That's what happens when there's not enough, shall we say *tender feelings*, between the Silver and the person they're fixing to turn.'

Quick's grimace increased.

'Sure, look at me like I'm a monster,' Monty said. 'It's your funeral. Or not, because you've probably guessed by now that we're not really in the business of bothering with last rites. Either way, if you decide to hate me, the Casting won't work, and you'll be *gone* by the weekend.'

'I didn't decide to hate you,' she said acidly. '*You* decided when you brought me here.'

Monty shook her, thumping her head back against the porch railings before pinning her there once more. 'It's my neck on the line here, too, you know,' he hissed. 'You think I'm not going to look a fool if I can't turn you? So just drop the hostility, all right? You were practically drooling at me back at the bar, so why can't you just do that again?'

'I didn't know you were a vampire back then. Or that you were… like this. And I was drunk.'

'I can get you drunk,' Monty offered.

'But you can't take back the rest.'

'Then what *can* I do?'

Quick looked at his beautiful face, his flawless skin, his shining eyes, but she could no longer find in his features the friendly barman who'd served her three nights ago, and for so many weeks previously during her searches for Evita. A few days ago, she'd looked at him and seen a way out of her misery, if just for a moment. Perhaps he had been no more than a consolation prize to her, but Quick had *wanted* the man she'd thought he was. Now that man was just… gone.

But he did still have one thing she wanted.

Needed.

'You can tell me about Evita,' she said.

Monty went still. He glanced at the porch door, then looked around carefully before lowering his voice even further to say, 'Gesture of goodwill?'

'At the very least, it might make me hate you less.'

'And that would be good for both of us,' he said calculatingly.

'Right.'

He licked his lips nervously, clearly caught in indecision, and Quick was reminded how young he was. What an idiot she'd been to follow him out here. Really, what had she been expecting? Not a vampire, certainly, but the idea that this kid would have anything useful to tell her, or any allure that was worth risking her flight home over, let alone her life—

But she couldn't think that way. If she did, apparently she was dead.

Then Monty whispered, 'You should be asking about Jane.' He spoke so quietly that Quick found herself involuntarily squinting to make out the words, as though that was going to help.

'Pardon me?'

'Jane,' Monty repeated. 'Not Evita. *Never* Evita, not in this house. Got it?'

'I don't—'

But then he was dragging her away from the railing, up the porch steps and through the house's glass doors, following the others into what appeared in the light of day to be a large and rather quaintly-appointed breakfast room. There were spindly little chairs arrayed next to spindly little side tables, and along one side of the room there was a breakfast buffet laid out on a table that was polished to such a perfect golden sheen that it had to be an antique. But none of that was dazzling enough to distract her from the line of people chained to the wall next to it.

'Monty—'

He shoved her up against the wall, knocking the breath out of her lungs, then she felt the metal click around her wrists.

By the time she recovered herself enough to do more than bend over and gasp for air, Monty and his fellow vampires had gone, leaving her and the others chained to the wall in a line. Xiaoyu was standing next to her.

'Don't fight it,' she whispered.

Quick blinked up at her through watering eyes, not understanding what she meant.

'Whatever happens next,' Xiaoyu clarified. 'Don't fight it.'

'*You're* telling me not to fight?'

Xiaoyu shrugged a shoulder. 'It goes easier if you don't.'

Over the next couple of hours, Quick was able to observe the truth of that in gruesome detail. People came into the room regularly, sometimes humans who took fruit and pastries from the buffet, sometimes vampires who ate their fill of the food, then pinned one of the chained humans back against the wall and bit into their necks with a chillingly casual directness. When her fellow offerings let it happen without protest, it was brief and efficient. When they fought – and only one did, a young man who was as new to the cellar as Quick – the protracted, screaming struggle finally ended with blood on the walls and a mauled wound at the boy's neck that was even more ragged than Quick's zombie bite.

The others looked away. That was the worst of it, and the thing that turned Quick's stomach when she remembered it later. As the boy screamed and thrashed against the wall in the grip of the vampire's jaws, the rest of the humans – Quick included – did nothing at all. *It was his own fault*, they muttered afterwards. They'd warned him not to fight it.

Every time someone new entered the room, Quick flinched, anticipating her own turn. She dipped her chin, hiding her face, trying to put off the inevitable, but there were only so many humans chained to the wall, and the vampires were avoiding those who'd already been bitten. After an hour, most of them had taken their turn; it was just Quick, Xiaoyu and one of the younger women at the far end of the line remaining. Odds were one in three that she'd be next.

'Fresh meat,' Bella yelled, coming in from the porch with a line of people following on behind her, including a few Quick recognised from the cellar. Bella and a couple of other vampires guided them into the room, then started unchaining the people who'd been brought in along with Quick. For one beautiful, shiny moment, Quick thought maybe they'd all get a reprieve, that she'd be allowed to return to the relative safety of the cellar unbitten, but when she looked at Xiaoyu, she was shaking her head. *Not until we're bled*, she mouthed.

And so it proved to be. The vampires were just switching out the people who'd already been bitten. The rest of them – Quick, Xiaoyu and the young woman at the other end of the line – stayed put as the others were unchained around them. A door opened across the room during the shuffle, and there was the noise of someone entering the space, but Quick's view was blocked by the exiting humans. It was only when they finally parted like clouds that she could see who had come in: the woman with the sunshine hair who walked like she was ready for a fight.

And Quick began to hope.

However fondly Quick was supposed to be thinking of him, she knew that Monty had precious little to offer her. If her fate rested on being able to conjure up the feelings she'd had for him on Tuesday night, then she was fucked. Monty was not Quick's way out of this place.

Her, though? The woman with the undercut and the determined look in her eye? She was an outsider here, too.

Quick could tell from the way she'd held herself at the party the other night. She hadn't been here to socialise, she'd come for a fight. Now she was Quick's last hope of salvation. Maybe somehow, Quick could appeal to her humanity and—

Then Quick met the woman's eyes, and she saw nothing but silver.

16

KULIKA WAS HUNGRY.

She'd ignored the thirst yesterday, and she'd made it through the night without losing too much sleep over it, but when she'd woken that morning and looked up at the spider-infested canopy above her head, she'd felt the weakness in her muscles and started to despair. For Kulika, who had practised discipline religiously since leaving this house a century ago, the sensation was a shameful surprise, but even her self-awareness couldn't stop the wanting.

She needed blood. She shouldn't, not so soon, not when she'd been using so little energy, and yet. Maybe it was all the bloodshed she'd witnessed two nights previously at the ritual. Maybe it was the constant state of fight-or-flight, or the memories swirling around her of the blood she'd spilled in this place, but all at once her devolution felt inevitable. Even her silver was slipping, the concealment of the colour in her eyes becoming impossible to sustain.

That hadn't been a problem for centuries. It would have been embarrassing in other circumstances. As it was, every Silver she encountered on her way from her suite to the breakfast room took the flashing of her silver as a threat, and got the hell out of her way, fast. She wondered then what they'd heard about her. Bartholomew wouldn't even have had to lie to make them fear her. They should. Right now, thirsting for blood in a place where drinking from the vein was her only option, Kulika feared herself.

As she barrelled into the breakfast room, she could smell the sugar on the pastries, the sweetness of the fruit, and the rich tang of blood flowing in the veins of the humans who were being chained along the wall. Now, the thirst was becoming irresistible in a way she recognised far too well, here in the very place where her thirst had plagued her most. She could feel her control slipping, inch by inch, in a way that would never have happened at home.

She could hear anxious hearts racing. She could smell the heat of blood rushing. If she looked very closely, she could even see arteries pulsing under the skin of the humans gathered against the wall, some already bitten, some bleeding from cuts that were more savage than they should have been. The new Silver led the drained ones away, shutting the porch door behind them.

Then Kulika saw her.

There, at the end of the line, was the woman with the hair like sunset. The woman who smelled like all the seasons kaleidoscoping into one. The new Silver had been blocking Kulika's view when she'd first entered the room, otherwise she would have noticed her immediately. She couldn't help herself from noticing her now, or from staring at her uncontrollably. Someone had already bitten her, judging from the marks on her neck. Then Kulika saw the mangled wound on the woman's arm and realised it must have been more than one someone. The Silver didn't bite like that.

'Who did this to you?' Kulika asked softly, stepping towards the woman.

She banished her weakness in a second, suppressing her silver, feeling her control locking into place once more.

It was too late, though. The woman had seen the silver.

'You're one of them,' she said with disgust.

Kulika's heart sank.

'One of *them*?' Kulika repeated stupidly, hoping against hope that the sunset-haired woman thought she was one of Bartholomew's crew. That, she could deny. And god, how she wanted to deny it. Anything not to be whoever *them* was.

But then…

'The vampires,' the sunset-haired woman said. 'You've got the silver veins in your eyes.'

There was no denying that.

'What did you think she was?' asked another of the chained-up humans, the woman from the cellar beneath the block, the one who'd spoken to Kulika the other day. Then the woman turned to Kulika and said, 'Are you going to tell us who you are, or what?'

'Kulika,' Kulika said.

'Xiaoyu,' the woman replied. 'This is Quick.' She went on to introduce the others, each by name, but Kulika had stopped listening the moment she'd heard that word.

Quick.

Even her name was an imperative. Kulika wanted to take it as an order. She could hear the thudding of Quick's heart — *Quick* — and she could feel the heat of her skin, even from across the distance that separated them. Kulika wanted to close the gap between them so keenly that it made her ache. Maybe it was just the thirst, and the exhaustion, and that beguiling scent of citrus and forests and frost, but she was now finding it impossible to restrain herself. Her gaze raked Quick's body uncontrollably, from the roots of her sunset hair to the tips of her bare toes, drinking in everything in between just as hungrily as Kulika wished she could drink in her scent, her taste, her blood.

Just a drop.

Without meaning to, Kulika took a step, and another, and who knew where she would have stopped if Xiaoyu hadn't interrupted by saying, 'I wasn't asking your name, though.'

Kulika blinked, and found Quick looking back at her with something close to horror, a horror that Kulika shared.

'I was asking who you *are*,' Xiaoyu continued. 'What you're doing here. When you're going to get us out of here, and why exactly you want to do that since you're one of *them*.'

'I'm not one of them,' Kulika said numbly. Her mind flashed back to the bloody carnage of two nights ago and her stomach churned. 'I'm Silver, yes,' she clarified. 'But these aren't my people.'

'They're feeding you,' Xiaoyu pointed out. 'And not just pastries.'

'Us,' Quick said quietly.

Kulika couldn't stand the vitriolic look on her face.

'He doesn't do that for just anyone,' Xiaoyu added.

'He?' Quick asked.

'Bartholomew,' Xiaoyu explained to her. 'The guy in charge. Head vampire. Coven leader. Whatever.'

'Captain,' Kulika said, then for reasons she couldn't explain even to herself, she told them the truth. 'Captain Bartholomew Roberts. I'm not sworn to him anymore, but a long time ago, a very long time ago, he made me part of his crew.'

'His *what*?' Xiaoyu asked, but Kulika paid little attention to her question because Quick was laughing.

Laughing.

'Bartholomew Roberts?' she asked, her eyebrows raised in

disbelief. 'Barti Ddu? You're telling me this place is owned by Black Bart, the infamous Golden Age pirate, and not only is he still alive, but he's a *vampire*?' Then she started laughing again, then crying, and finally she slumped back against the wall with her face hidden behind her sunset-red hair.

'Don't mind her,' said Xiaoyu. 'She's new.'

But Kulika did mind. She minded a lot.

The confused scent coming off Quick wasn't so much frost and sunshine now as it was bitter leaves and wet earth, muted and fallow, as though her scent were an extension of her mood. Kulika had never come across a scent that changed like that before, and she wasn't sure what it meant.

'Are you okay?' Kulika asked, taking one restrained step closer to Quick.

'Is it true?' Quick asked, her face still hidden by her hair.

'Yes,' Kulika said, standing in front of her, but still a good six feet away, for everyone's safety. 'Didn't you know? You signed his covenant, so I thought—'

Then Quick tossed her hair away from her face and looked up at Kulika. Her eyes were so green. Green like grass, but not the grass here in the baking summer of South Carolina, the grass back home where only the hottest days of the hottest summers parched it from rich to dull.

'What are you talking about?' Quick asked.

'The Articles,' said Kulika. 'He said you signed the Articles.' Then Kulika glanced around Quick's body to where her hands were chained to the wall, and saw her unblemished palms. 'You're not wearing his black mark.'

'What are you talking about?'

'The ones in the blood cellar don't sign until we get turned,' Xiaoyu said.

Which meant Bartholomew had lied to her, Kulika

realised. The night when she'd arrived back at the mansion and Bartholomew had offered Quick to her, saying she'd signed his covenant… Well, she hadn't. Quick wasn't wearing Bartholomew's mark, and she wasn't Bartholomew's to trade with. Which meant she wasn't Bartholomew's to claim, either.

Oh, Kulika thought.

Oh.

The ramifications of that knowledge were dangerous. *Very* dangerous.

Perhaps it was just the thirst talking, but Kulika *wanted* Quick. She could break her chains without effort, even blood-starved as she was. She could walk out of here, fight her way through the guards and take Quick with her, and Bartholomew wouldn't be able to do a thing about it.

Not a single thing.

Except deny Kulika the knowledge that had brought her here in the first place, knowledge that would save the woman Baron Drake loved. Knowledge that would save him too, the only man who had proved himself worthy of the loyalty she gave him.

Kulika loved him. It was a platonic, dutiful, unspoken kind of love, but it was real. That was what she was weighing against the freedom of a single human she'd just met.

It was an easy reckoning, or at least it should have been.

'You're thirsty,' Xiaoyu said, interrupting Kulika's muddled thoughts.

'What?'

'I said, you're thirsty. You need blood.'

'I… No, I'm fine,' Kulika insisted, ignoring the way her muscles twitched with need. It came over her like this sometimes, the thirst, when she'd been over-exerting and under-consuming. It felt like acidosis shaking and tingling through her thighs, making them spasm ever so slightly beyond her control.

'If you were fine, then you wouldn't be looking at Quick like you're an alcoholic and she's a fifth of bourbon. Here,' Xiaoyu said, turning her head to tip her hair away from the side of her neck. 'Drink.'

'No,' Kulika said, horrified, but whether the horror stemmed from the idea of the act itself, now it came down to it, or from the identity of the donor, she wasn't sure. She couldn't remember the last time she'd drunk from the vein. Well, actually she could, and that was rather the problem. 'I don't—'

'You said you were going to get us out of here,' Xiaoyu said. 'Right?'

'I said I would try,' Kulika replied carefully.

When she'd made that promise, she'd had no idea how she'd keep it, and that hadn't changed. Sneaking out of here with Quick was one thing, but there were more than a hundred humans in that cellar, and she was just one Silver against Bartholomew's entire empire. She had no chance.

'Well, on the off-chance that you're telling the truth, you can't help us if you're shaking like that, can you?' Xiaoyu said.

'Shaking?' Quick asked, looking at Kulika with concern. Kulika saw her attention settling on Kulika's fingers – steady as a rock – before settling on her thighs. She looked down to see that there was a faint, but unfortunately visible, twitching in her legs.

'I'm fine,' Kulika said again, because quite apart from the memories she was trying to suppress, she could see the many overlaid scars patterning Xiaoyu's neck. She could hear the erratic faintness of her pulse, too, and scent the sickly deficits in her blood. She had been fed from too much, and for too long. 'You're not, though. You can't spare the blood.'

'I'm fine,' said Xiaoyu brusquely, but she leaned forward so her hair curtained back over her shoulders, hiding the scars at her throat.

'I can spare it,' said Quick resolutely, offering her own neck.

Kulika's mouth went dry. Her eyes traced Quick's freckled skin with her gaze, from the soft curve of her shoulder, along her collar bone, to the point where the vein thudded in her elegant neck. Kulika would kill to taste her blood, but in this urgent state she might end up doing exactly that.

'No,' Kulika finally croaked, with effort.

'Then one of the others,' Xiaoyu said, nodding towards the humans lined up beside her. Some of them were watching the three women with mild interest, but others were eyeing up the buffet, or slumping against the wall as though lost in thought, but probably just too exhausted to move. They were all grim, they were all dirty, and none of them spoke a word except Quick and Xiaoyu.

It was eerie.

Kulika hesitated. Maybe she could go out into the city somehow, maybe find a blood bank or—

The door opened behind her, and she turned to see Bartholomew leaning casually in the doorway. She wondered how long he'd been hanging around outside, listening, waiting.

'Still not drinking?' he asked. It was a taunt.

'Not thirsty,' she lied.

He barked a single, sharp laugh. 'Still so hesitant, Kulika? Chasing ghosts? I thought you'd have put them to rest decades ago.'

He knew exactly what was haunting her. He'd been here

when Kulika had taken her last bite, and there when she'd taken her first bite, and present for every one in between. He'd always been there, watching, and here he was still. She'd been naïve to expect anything else.

She turned to face him, trying her best to mask the muscle spasms in her legs, but of course he saw. He *always* saw.

Then his gaze passed along the line of humans and he saw Quick. His eyes widened, just slightly, so slightly that most Silver probably wouldn't even have noticed the reaction, but his surprise and displeasure was clear enough to someone who had known him as long as Kulika had.

He was trying to hide it from her, but he was angry.

He turned and yelled out into the hall: 'Get the kid in here. Now!'

When "the kid" arrived, he proved to be the same boy who'd interrupted her conversation with Bartholomew on her first evening at the mansion: Mr Monteiro.

'What is this one doing here?' Bartholomew asked him, pointing at Quick.

'She's new,' the kid said, bewildered. 'The new ones do the feeds.'

Bartholomew grabbed the kid roughly around the back of the neck and pulled him close, pressing his forehead against the kid's, staring down into his eyes. The old pirate whispered, 'Why must you disappoint me like this?'

'I didn't— I thought—'

'Did I not make your duty clear?'

Kulika could see Bartholomew's grip tightening around the kid's scruff, his fingers whitening as they dug into his flesh. The kid's mouth screwed into a line of pain, but he didn't try to escape. He was wearing Bartholomew's mark on his palm, and there was no escaping that.

'I'm sorry,' the kid gritted out. 'I'll fix it.'

'See that you do,' Bartholomew said. He stared into the kid's eyes for one last second before letting him free, dropping the kid from his grip as though he were a louse he'd picked out of his hair.

The moment he was released, the kid ran for Quick and started fumbling with her chains. Kulika wanted to stop him. She wanted to scream and fight and stand in his way, but with Bartholomew standing right there, she couldn't afford to show any emotion at all. If he saw a crack in her defences, he'd slip his fingers inside it and twist until it broke her open, so instead of going after what she wanted, she stood and watched impassively while the young Silver freed Quick from the wall and started dragging her towards the porch doors, dragging her away from Kulika.

Then Quick lunged. The kid couldn't have been expecting it. With his Silver strength, it should have been laughably easy to keep a human under control, but nonetheless Quick's wrists slipped from his grip, and his surprise gave her enough time to launch herself at Kulika.

Quick thudded into Kulika's chest like a key thrusting into the lock it was made to fit. Her sudden presence in Kulika's arms was overwhelming – her warmth, her scent, the softness of her skin – so overwhelming that Kulika lost her breath along with her mind, and found herself unable to say anything at all. She should have been pushing her back, pretending Quick's proximity did nothing to her, but instead she just looked down into Quick's green eyes and began to swim.

Until Quick spoke.

'I need to ask you about Jane,' she whispered urgently, as though the name was one Kulika should recognise.

'Jane?'

'Jane. I need to find her, to find—'

Then the kid grabbed Quick by the wrist and jerked her back, out of Kulika's arms, out of the porch doors and away. The abruptness of it was numbing, leaving Kulika with nothing but the twitching of her muscles and the cold, sick sensation that something that was part of her had been lost.

The strength of her reaction was an unwelcome surprise, one she tried to cover by asking Bartholomew, 'Who's Jane?'

Kulika hadn't forgotten what she'd overheard the first night she'd been here, or how Bartholomew had reacted when the kid had told him, *I think she knows Jane.* She wondered now if he'd been talking about Quick. Bartholomew had certainly been unsettled to find Quick here, in exactly the same way he had been unsettled when he'd heard her say Jane's name, however much he was trying to hide it now.

'She's just one of the many new Silver we've welcomed to the mansion over the past six months,' Bartholomew replied dismissively, but he was schooling his expression in a way that just made Kulika more suspicious. 'No one special. And there are more to come tonight. You'll attend the Casting ceremony, of course.' It was an order, not an enquiry.

'And the human you just had taken away?' Kulika said, prodding. 'You seemed a little upset to see her here.'

'If I am upset,' Bartholomew replied, 'then it's because a member of my crew failed to follow orders. The girl is irrelevant.' He smiled. It put Kulika on edge. 'Unless you were planning to make a meal of her yourself? But perhaps I can offer you an alternative.'

He walked to the wall and snatched one of the young women out of the line, breaking the chains that held her in place. She hadn't been bitten yet today, or at all in fact, if her unblemished throat was any clear measure. She was a redhead, but her hair was more strawberry blonde than auburn, with none of the sunset fire of Quick's.

'Get the other humans out of here!' Bartholomew yelled into the hall, and a couple of young Silver rushed in to do as he demanded, leaving just the three of them behind in the breakfast room: Bartholomew, Kulika and the strawberry blonde.

Bartholomew pushed the woman into Kulika's arms, pressing in behind so she was trapped between the two of them. Kulika tried to move back, but Bartholomew chased her every step of the way, until her back was against the wall and there was nowhere to run. With the woman's vein thrumming so close to her mouth, she was no longer certain that she wanted to.

'Do you think I can't see the need in you?' Bartholomew whispered to Kulika over the young woman's shoulder, leaning in so close that Kulika could feel his lips moving against her earlobe. 'You can't hide your appetites from me. I know your hunger too well. You remember what happened the night you left?'

As if she could ever forget.

It had been months of deprivation, months of punishment for what Bartholomew had termed her *little mutinies*, all designed to push her to the edge until she snapped. *I can't be lenient with you just because you're my second*, he'd explained over and over as he drained and starved her of blood. *If I don't discipline you for your little mutinies, when you're supposed to be the most loyal of all my crew, then what will become of my authority? You brought this upon yourself.*

She'd nodded, and apologised, and begged his forgiveness for being late to answer his call, or for failing to pass on every tiny piece of gossip she overheard from the crew, or for punishing them more leniently than he would have liked for their transgressions. In those last months, there had always been some new crime for which he demanded her atonement. She could see now exactly how he'd manipulated her into that final crisis, but that awareness did nothing to limit her shame.

When she'd bitten the girl, and the many others that had followed in her rampage, she hadn't been in her right mind. Not that it mattered. Bartholomew would have used her guilt to tie her to him ever more inextricably, and if Baron Drake hadn't been there to get her out when he did…

He'd barely known her back then, but he'd seen enough during his visit to the mansion to know that Bartholomew had broken her and, for some reason that Kulika still didn't fully understand to this day, he'd decided to help her instead of condemning her. Maybe he'd seen something of his own savagery in her and felt a kinship there, because he was certainly capable of savagery himself. Or maybe he'd seen someone who needed to be rescued, and decided to play the white knight for once. Either way, he'd cleaned up the mess she'd left in her wake, forcing Bartholomew to relinquish his claim on her under threat of mortal retaliation. In doing so, he'd put his position and his life on the line, irreparably fracturing the uneasy alliance between the Silver of the UK and those of the USA in the process. It was a debt she could never repay, but she could at least try, and god knew she'd been doing a crap job of that so far.

'I see you shaking, Kulika,' Bartholomew said, grabbing the human between them by the back of her head to tilt her chin back and bare her neck to Kulika's bite. 'You're weak. If you mean to last through the weekend and get the information you came here for, then you need to drink. So drink. I know you like a redhead. I haven't forgotten the way you looked at Penny on the night you arrived.'

Kulika had no idea who Penny was, but with the young woman's blood just a breath away, she was struggling to remember her own name, let alone anyone else's.

'It's the only way we feed in this mansion,' Bartholomew said. 'Not from bottles or bags, stored and tainted with plastic. My crew drinks only the best, fresh and warm and straight from the vein, as we always have. You can feel the power in it, can't you?'

To her shame, she could. She remembered it from every dream she'd had since she left this mansion. Sometimes they were nightmares, but sometimes…

Kulika's vision was beginning to strobe, narrowing her senses so that when Bartholomew leaned down to the young woman's neck and sank his teeth into her throat, opening a vein that dripped tantalising streaks of red down over her skin, all Kulika could see, smell, feel, *taste* in the air was the blood.

Bartholomew pulled back, then he reached out his free hand to wrap around the back of Kulika's head, settling it at the base of her skull as though it belonged there, guiding her to the thing that – in that moment – she wanted more than anything in the world.

Kulika was lost before her lips were even wet, drinking as though her thirst were just as acute as it had been back then, after Bartholomew had starved her, instead of being a minor inconvenience she could have controlled with enough discipline. She told herself that drinking the woman's blood was a concession she was making to save Baron Drake's life, that if she didn't then she would weaken into uselessness, or Bartholomew would evict her from the mansion with no information at all about Evita Khalyed's whereabouts. But the truth she knew in her heart was that she should have been able to last days, weeks, perhaps even months without drinking again and still function well enough to fulfil her purpose, which was simply a matter of remaining in the mansion until Monday arrived. The truth was, she'd allowed Bartholomew to influence her, just as he had done a hundred years before, and for all the hundreds of years before that.

She was weak, and she had allowed him to break her. Again.

As she pulled away from the young woman's neck, leaving behind a double bite mark that was as clean as she could make it, but still not clean enough, Kulika felt the blood settling in her stomach like a rock.

Bartholomew smiled wolfishly and said, 'It's good to have you back.'

17

'JANE,' QUICK SAID desperately, 'I need to find her, to find—'

But then there were hands around Quick's wrists, shoving her out through the doors and down the porch steps, hurrying her bare feet over the flagstones around the pool, leaving her with nothing but the memory of Kulika's baffled expression.

She hadn't recognised the name. Whatever Kulika's true purpose was in this house – and Quick realised then that she never had told them – she clearly had no idea who Jane was.

'You're a liability,' Monty hissed at her as he dragged her to one of the poolside chairs and sat her down in it.

'And you're a liar,' Quick replied.

'You couldn't wait more than a couple of hours before blurting out that name? If I'd known you were that impatient —'

'What was that about in there?' Quick asked. 'What did you do wrong? I wasn't supposed to be bitten, was I?'

'Please, just… stop,' was the only reply she received.

Moments later, the other human captives were hurried out of the breakfast room behind them, and Monty handed Quick off to the vampires who were escorting them, as though he

150

couldn't wait to be rid of her. He barely looked at her. It didn't bode well for tonight.

'Jane?' one of the humans whispered as they were all shepherded across the lawn on their way back to the block. The speaker was a man walking just ahead of her who looked to be about her age, with matted shoulder-length hair that might have started out in braids. 'Why was the new girl asking about Jane?'

'Shut up,' Xiaoyu whispered quickly, and he duly shut up. Not quickly enough, though. Between one step and the next, Bella – who was among their escort – aimed a kick at his knee, an economical gesture that looked like nothing at all, but ended in a stomach-churning snap that had the man pitching forward and onto the ground with a scream that made Quick's skin shiver.

'We don't talk about Jane,' Bella said, then she walked off ahead with the others, leaving Xiaoyu and the woman she'd called Reynolds to pull the injured man to his feet and help him, still yelling, across the lawn. Quick fell in step beside them, hovering there in case she was needed, but feeling utterly useless as the vampires and the other humans walked swiftly back inside the distant block, leaving them behind.

Quick saw Reynolds's fear as she looked anxiously towards the door of the building, and guessed this would not end well for any of them. The man was still screaming.

'Shh,' Xiaoyu said urgently to him. 'Come on. We've just got to get you inside—'

'I'm sorry,' said Reynolds, then she dropped the man's arm from around her shoulders and made a break for the block at a flat run, slipping through the metal side door as Quick scrambled to take her place.

'For fuck's sake, shut up,' Xiaoyu said as the man screamed.

'Xiaoyu!' Quick rebuked her.

'If we don't get him inside quickly and quietly then we're all— Too late,' she said, her eyes widening as she looked beyond the trees.

The vampires were coming back. Three of them, striding out of the building towards Quick, Xiaoyu, and the man who couldn't walk even with their help.

'We've got him,' Xiaoyu insisted. 'We can take him.'

They ignored her entirely. One scooped the man into his arms while the other two held Xiaoyu and Quick back. What happened next was the work of a moment: a bite, a twist, and then the vampire was carrying the man's body across the gardens towards the river that glinted at the distant edge of the property.

'For the gators,' the vampire who was holding Xiaoyu explained, grinning at Quick's dismay.

'Fucking Bella,' said the other from behind Quick. 'Someone's got to get her under control. Isn't this one Monty's?' He shook Quick a little, as though she were nothing but a prop.

'Want me to go get him?' asked the other.

'I'll go. You got them in the meantime?'

The other laughed, as though the idea of him being unable to control a couple of humans was ridiculous.

'Yeah, okay,' said the one holding Quick as he passed her to the other. 'Be right back.'

He rushed off to the block, moving so fast that Quick could barely see him. She caught her breath and whispered to Xiaoyu, 'Is that speed normal?'

Then there was a clatter from the mansion behind them, the porch doors opened and the last human stumbled out, a redheaded young woman, holding her neck. She collapsed on the porch steps.

'Fuck's sake,' the last Silver muttered. 'Not another one.' He pushed Quick and Xiaoyu down onto the grass, said, 'Sit. Stay,' then rushed off to fetch the redhead while Quick and Xiaoyu looked on silently from their spot on the lawn.

'Well,' whispered Xiaoyu. 'There goes our last hope of getting out of here before tonight.'

'What?' said Quick.

'Kulika, or whatever her name is. The point is, she was lying.'

'Because she drank from that girl? Come on, Xiaoyu. You offered her your blood, didn't you? Just because she bit her, it doesn't mean—'

'Look at her neck,' said Xiaoyu as the girl was carried past. Quick did, reluctantly, and what she saw made her wince. The girl's throat had been mauled with more than one bite, breaking her skin in a way that reminded Quick of the boy who'd struggled. It was a mess.

'Face facts: she's not here to save us,' Xiaoyu said quietly. 'She's just another one of them. If we're going to get out of here, then we're going to have to do it on our own.'

'I don't suppose there's any point in running?' Quick said.

'From here? In the daylight? With vamps all around us? No. We do it when they're not expecting it, at night—'

'Because that worked out so well for you last time,' said a sarcastic voice from behind them. Quick turned to see Monty coming around the pool from the far side of the house, trailing a couple of other Silver in his wake. 'You're not going anywhere, Xiaoyu. You've tried, like, twenty times. Give up.'

Xiaoyu was glaring at Monty. The fierceness in her eyes suggested there was more to their past than Quick had realised.

'But as it happens,' Monty continued, 'Quick *is* going

somewhere.'

'Oh?' Xiaoyu asked. When Xiaoyu glanced her way, Quick could see the concern in her eyes.

'Come on, sugar,' Monty said to Quick, grabbing her by the wrist and pulling her to her feet. 'We're going upstairs.' Then he wrapped his arm around Quick's shoulders with a casualness that suggested she should welcome it.

There were wolf whistles and laughs from the Silver, but Quick was left with little doubt that she *absolutely* did not want to go upstairs with Monty. She made to push him away, but he sank his fingers into her shoulder and held her close, whispering into her ear, 'Am I really worse than turning zombie?'

In that moment, with shivers of disgust travelling up her spine, Quick honestly wasn't sure. She looked at Xiaoyu's anxious face and the words she'd said to Quick earlier that day returned in a dark echo.

Don't fight it.

It goes easier if you don't.

For better or worse, Quick didn't. She let Monty take her inside the block with Xiaoyu and the others trailing along behind, and tried to find the strength to make herself yield.

18

THE ONSLOW.
> *The Royal Fortune.*
> *The Porcupine.*

So many names tattooed down Kulika's spine, across her heart and into her bones. Bartholomew might have forgotten them, but Kulika would not. By the time this trip was over, if indeed it ever ended, she would have many more names to add to the list.

> *The cellar.*
> *The redhead.*
> *Quick.*

So many people she'd failed. So many lives she'd traded to get what she needed. But what was the alternative? Do nothing? Just walk away empty-handed and let the baron die?

That she could not do.

Just three more nights. She just had to wait until Monday, then Bartholomew would give her the information she came here to get. Just three more nights, then she could track down Evita Khalyed, turn her Silver, and take her back to Oxford, where the science bods could use her blood to make an antidote to save stupid Jack's stupid life, ensuring that Baron Drake's rather more precious life would continue for centuries to come.

That was why she'd come here, she reminded herself. That was why she was enduring Bartholomew's games. She just had to concentrate on her own mission, instead of letting herself get distracted by the allures of… other things. She was a soldier now, not some rebel pirate who could follow her own whims.

Discipline, that's what she needed, for tonight and everything that would follow. *Discipline*, she repeated in her head as she leaned on the porch railing and tried to steel herself against the carnage that would surely come at the Casting that evening.

She could still taste the woman's blood in her mouth, sharp and fearful. In her muddled senses, it leaked into the tantalising scent of four seasons rolled into one, souring to bitter leaves. Her mind was filled with memories of a soft body pressed against her own, memories of her teeth sinking into flesh she didn't want to bite, that had already been bitten by another, marred by the saliva of the person she hated more than anyone in the world. She'd tasted him in the woman's blood. Part of him was inside Kulika now, not just the blood that had turned her into what she was today, but his *spit*.

After all the violations Bartholomew had perpetrated against her, how strange it was that her mind had latched onto that one to stoke her outrage.

'You drank from the vein, then,' Bayly said, coming to stand beside her in his spot, just as he always did. 'Wasn't sure you would.'

Kulika didn't want to talk about it, particularly not with Bayly. What business did he have judging her, with the mess he'd gotten himself into? But she knew his judgement wouldn't chafe were it not for the fact that she agreed with his censure.

It had been... undisciplined, and that worried her. If Bartholomew was set on breaking her down piece by piece, then so far he was succeeding. Kulika knew that he would only stop when she'd signed his Articles, and Baron Drake wasn't here to bargain her out of them this time. She couldn't afford to let Bartholomew mark her with his covenant again.

She'd burned the first black spot out of her skin in the bowels of a ship bound for England, holding her palm against the boiler until it puckered and smoked as she'd screamed into the din of the engine room. When she'd ripped her hand away, the scalding metal had claimed the tainted skin. It was a rebirth in fire, even if that fire was blackened by coal dust and soot.

Kulika was a phoenix, she reminded herself. A hundred years ago, she'd bid good riddance to those ashes and – whatever Bartholomew thought her biting that woman symbolised – she would rise from them once more.

'It's no concern of yours what I do,' she said to Bayly as she pushed away from the railing and headed back into the house. 'You said it yourself: we're no longer on the same crew.'

19

FROM THE ROOF of the block, the view over the river was beautiful. Quick and Monty were up above the shade of the trees, but there was a covered deck that faced east, sheltering them from the worst of the afternoon sun and giving them as much privacy as they could have wished for. In other circumstances, it might even have been romantic, but not now, not here, when Quick knew exactly what was going on in the building beneath them.

In the cellar in the bowels of the block, she knew that Xiaoyu and the others were waiting to see which of them would get dragged out for the Casting and which would stay in the blood bank until they were used up. Monty had walked her through the rest of the block on their way up here to the roof, giving her the tour. The ground floor was innocuous enough: the wash rooms, the kitchen, store rooms, the wardrobe, and some messy common areas that were filled with vampires watching TV, playing video games and generally hanging out. They could have been plucked out of any college campus across the country. The dorm rooms on the upper two floors of the building would have had a similar college feel to them, had it not been for the rampant orgy going on within them. Quick hadn't known where to look.

'It can be fun here,' Monty had said to her unabashedly.

Quick had squinted along the corridor filled with half-naked people spilling from one room to another, laughing and screaming and moaning, and thought it didn't *sound* fun. It sounded like intoxication and mania and desperation.

'Are they on drugs?' she'd asked.

Whatever he'd expected her reaction to be, it hadn't been that.

'They want to be here, Quick,' he'd said irritably. 'Most of these people begged to be allowed up here. They're desperate just for the chance to be like us. Do you not understand that? Do you not understand how lucky you are? It's here or in the cellar. You can be up here and enjoy yourself, or you can die down there in the dark.'

'Lucky?' she'd said incredulously. 'Lucky that you kidnapped me and bit me and brought me here against my will to bet my life for the chance to become a monster? Why would I *want* that?'

That's when he'd lost it, dragging her up the concrete staircase at the end of the hall and through the fire door that led out onto the roof. For a moment, she'd thought he was going to throw her right off it, but then he'd stopped and sat down on the deck, huffing like an overly-dramatic teenager. Which was practically what he was, Quick realised.

'I didn't choose this either, you know,' he said now. 'I didn't ask to be this way. Well, I did, but not in the way you might imagine.'

Quick sighed, because of course Monty was going to make this about himself. Worse, he was going to make her drag it out of him like he was some brooding, reluctant love interest and she was his fawning admirer. Well, she didn't have time for that. She didn't have time for any of this nonsense, not if she was going to find a way out of this mess before the end of the night.

She plonked herself down next to him unceremoniously and said, 'Spill it.'

That was all the encouragement Monty needed to launch into his tragic story. He'd been the first of the new vampires, he claimed, turned by a man who was centuries old, yet apparently not wise enough to avoid falling head over heels for Monty. He'd promised Monty the secret of eternal life, a secret Monty desperately needed in order to save his poor dying mother, but when Monty had woken to his undeath and realised that eternal life came with the curse of drinking human blood, he knew his god-fearing mother would never accept it, or him, so here he was, doomed to live forever, unloved and bereft of family.

The whole story felt hollow and rehearsed, and Quick didn't believe a word of it.

'You didn't have to drag me into it,' she said when he was finished.

'We have to make more Silver,' he replied with a shrug. It was a nonchalant dismissal, which as good as acknowledged that he'd never taken her feelings into consideration, and he certainly wasn't about to start now.

'Why?'

'Bartholomew says so.'

Quick remembered everything she'd half-learned that morning about the vampire in charge – the *pirate* in charge – and wished she'd had a chance to ask more than the most cursory questions about who he was and why he was keeping them here. Then she remembered the imposing man who'd grabbed Monty by the scruff of his neck, and she started to put two and two together.

'You're talking about the man who made you unchain

me?' she asked.

'He really wants you to be Silver,' said Monty. 'Don't ask me why, because I don't have an answer for you, but he wants you to turn and he wants it to happen tonight.'

'Or else?'

Monty just shrugged again, but his expression said enough. He wasn't simply scared of Bartholomew Roberts, he was petrified.

'They killed that man,' Quick said.

'What man?'

'When we were on our way back here from the house, one of the guys who heard me talking about Jane mentioned her name, and Bella broke his leg. Shattered it, more like,' she added, remembering the noise it had made with sickening clarity.

'Oh,' Monty said. 'Yeah. I heard they took someone to the river.'

'Just for saying her name. You're the one who told me to ask about her.'

'I didn't tell you to ask *Bella*,' he said. 'She's out of her fucking mind. Just… stay away from her, okay?'

'No problem,' she said. 'Because I'm not going back down to the dorms.'

'You might want to,' Monty replied with what seemed like reluctance.

'Why?'

'It doesn't have to be me, Quick.'

Quick looked at him, puzzled, examining his face for some clue as to what he meant and finding none.

'There are a lot of Silver downstairs,' he said. 'Take your pick. I want it to be me who turns you, but it doesn't have to be. It can be any other Silver in this building.'

'Why on earth would you want it to be you?' Quick asked,

bewildered. 'After all this?'

'I'm the one who chose you,' he said, looking into her eyes as though he were trying to impart some deep feeling with his words. 'I didn't do that for nothing. I *like* you.'

'I liked you, too, Monty,' Quick replied. 'But then—'

'But then nothing,' he said, reaching out to cup her cheek with his hand. 'Forget the rest. Can we just go back to that night in the bar? Just for tonight, can you try to forget everything that happened after, for both of our sakes? We've only got until midnight.'

Quick hesitated, wanting to peel his palm from her cheek, but also realising that he was talking some twisted kind of sense.

'People stay together, you know,' he whispered. 'Afterwards.'

'You mean there are *couples* in that mess downstairs?'

'Not downstairs,' Monty admitted. 'They normally move out, into the city or around here. The boss is always happy to make arrangements for people to live close, once they've paid their debt, and if I turn you then my slate will be clean. He's got deep pockets, you know.'

'Is that what this is?' Quick asked, finally taking his hand from her cheek to trace the black mark on his palm with her fingertips. 'The mark of your debt?'

'No,' he replied. 'This is something else.'

'The covenant?'

He nodded, swallowing. 'That's… That's forever. But if I can turn you Silver, then he'll buy us a place together. Let us leave. Set us up in style, you know?'

'And that's a life you *want*?'

'Given all the choice in the world, maybe I'd choose different. But it's better than dying in the cellar, isn't it? And when you're Silver, I can tell you everything. Maybe we can even go looking for your friend together. How about that?'

That caught Quick's attention. It was the most attractive offer she'd had from him since they'd left the restaurant, and she couldn't imagine why he was making it.

'*You're* not going to die in the cellar,' she said, still trying – and failing – to understand what was motivating him.

'Maybe not down there, but…' He looked away for a moment, as though he were washing a thought from his mind. 'There are other ways to die in this place. That's why we're all doing this, Quick. We just want to get out alive. So I guess the question is: do you want to get out with me, or not? If it would help,' he said, pulling a small bottle of rum from his back pocket, 'I can even get you drunk.'

When he put it like that, with his eyes locked on hers in a way she remembered viscerally from that night in the bar, the offer was hard to refuse.

Don't fight it.

It goes easier if you don't.

Quick grabbed the bottle and drained it half empty, then handed it to Monty to finish. When he'd downed his portion, he threaded his fingers through Quick's and looked at her for a moment, waiting.

This was it, then.

Quick closed her eyes, picturing someone else beyond the shield of her eyelids, leaned in, and kissed him.

Don't fight it.

To save her own life, along with any hope she had of saving Evita's, she could force herself to yield.

20

AS MIDNIGHT APPROACHED, Kulika found herself in the middle of a full-blown, bells and blood, candles and incense Casting ceremony. Perhaps she shouldn't have been surprised, but somehow she hadn't expected the new crew to keep to the old rituals. They weren't actually necessary. All you needed to turn someone Silver was a blood exchange and an emotional link between the couple involved, so why bother with the chanting and the processions and all the bloody Latin? Kulika had assumed that a confirmed rebel like Bartholomew would avoid all the pomp and circumstance, as he had in his days of high seas piracy, so she was surprised when she left her room that night to find one of the human servants standing outside her door, offering her a robe.

And a phone.

'It's for you,' the man said.

Kulika looked at the screen and saw that there was an open line to an unlisted number. She took it suspiciously and held it to her ear.

'Hello?' she asked.

'It's Jack,' Baron Drake said, with no preamble. His voice

was shakier than she would have liked.

'What about her?' Kulika asked.

'She's running out of time.'

Kulika's grip tightened around the phone hard enough to make it creak. She took a deep breath, got herself under control and asked, 'How long have I got?'

'I don't know. The Primus, he… Look, I just need you to hurry. Are you getting anywhere?'

'Yes,' she lied. 'I should know where Khalyed is by Monday.'

'That's days away,' the baron said.

He let everything he'd left unsaid hang in the air between them.

It's too long.

Jack doesn't have time.

If Jack dies, then I die.

After a few empty seconds, Kulika said, 'I'll see what I can do,' then the line went dead.

Under normal circumstances, Kulika would have considered that suspicious, or at the very least a little rude, but then Bartholomew walked out of his own room next door, wearing his own robe, with a look on his face that was too innocent to be believed. Kulika was sure he'd at least been listening to her conversation with the baron, and in all probability he'd been controlling the line, waiting until he had what he wanted before cutting the call dead.

He knew how desperate she was now. Kulika had just given him a bargaining chip, and from the look on his face, he couldn't wait to play it.

'Something wrong?' he asked her lightly.

'You know what's wrong,' she replied, thrusting her hands into the arms of her robe and pulling up the hood. 'I can't wait until Monday. I need you tell tell me where Evita

Khalyed is. Now.'

'Oh dear.' Bartholomew's sincerity was entirely fake. He was a better actor than that, but he wasn't even trying now. 'Well, if you want to move up the schedule, perhaps you'd consider…' He pulled the large leather-bound book from within the folds of his voluminous robe and opened it to a new page, proffering it like a platter of delicacies.

'I'm not signing the Articles,' Kulika said.

'Not even for Jack?' Bartholomew asked with twinkling eyes. 'Yes, I know about her. I think the entire Silver world knows about Jack Valentine by now, the young fool who poisoned herself trying to kill the Primus and yet somehow, unaccountably, finds herself forgiven.'

Kulika winced inwardly. It was inevitable that the news would get out eventually, with the splash Jack had made with that particular piece of idiocy. Kulika could only hope that it wasn't yet common knowledge that Baron Drake had silvered for Jack, because once that news leaked, she'd be out of time. They all would be.

'What I don't understand,' Bartholomew went on, 'is why *you'd* care enough to try to save her, or what the woman you're searching for has to do with any of it. But if you'd care to explain to me—'

'This has nothing to do with Jack,' Kulika said, too quickly.

'Then why are you looking for her?'

'I do what I'm told.'

Bartholomew laughed. 'For *him*, perhaps.'

'And for you!' Kulika yelled, snapping. 'For hundreds of years, I did everything you told me. I buckled down, and buckled under, and tied myself in knots following your orders. All I'm asking for is a little grace. Give me the information I need, and I'll come back here after I've done what needs doing. You'll have the three days I owe you.'

'And you expect me to take your word for that? When you abandoned me and my covenant?' Bartholomew said, shaking his head like a disappointed parent. 'You know there's only one thing you can do to repair my trust.' He held out the book again, pulling a sharp-nibbed quill from his robes to lay across its pages. 'You want to surrender yourself to me just as much as I want you to,' he said, leaning in close. 'You belong here, Kulika. With me.'

The terrible thing was, part of her believed it, and every time he told her so, she believed it a little more. After everything she'd done, all the blood she'd spilled, and the blood she'd drunk from the vein of an unwilling human only that morning…

Didn't she belong here more than she belonged anywhere else?

That was the power Bartholomew had always wielded over her. He validated the darkest parts of her, the parts she kept hidden from the baron and everyone else in her neat little life across the Atlantic, and by validating them he turned her shame into his strength. He *knew* her. He knew the memories that plagued her, the urges she laboured under, and the way she would break if he pushed her in just the right way. Worse, he enjoyed those parts of her. He gloried in the wreckage she knew no one else would even tolerate if they knew it was there.

It would have been easier if he'd just wanted to destroy her. Instead, he wanted to release her darkest self and worship it. He had always loved the way she fell apart.

'Sign,' he whispered. 'And I'll give you everything you ask of me, for the rest of time.'

'No orders?' she asked.

'No orders,' he agreed. 'Except the ones you may give to

me. Do as I ask, and I shall be your slave.'

'No restrictions?'

'You leave Drake and stay here with your crew, where you belong. Other than that, no.'

'But you'll let me complete the mission I started for him?'

Bartholomew looked into her eyes for a long moment. She could see his reluctance, but it was matched by his hunger. Eventually, he said, 'Yes. Then return to me, and I will make you a pirate queen worthy of this crew. Worthy of *any* crew.'

Kulika weighed his words, and felt the truth in them.

The feelings they were holding between their locked gazes took on a dreamlike quality. He *wanted* her. Not romantically, not physically, but still so intensely that he – the fabled dread pirate Roberts – was was prepared to humble himself at her feet just to have her at his side. It was intoxicating. When she saw herself through his eyes, Kulika saw a goddess drenched in blood.

For a moment, she forgot that she had abandoned that self centuries ago. Trapped in the heat of his awe, Kulika picked up the quill and held it against her fingertip, poised to prick her blood onto the page.

Then a gong rang through the house, and the quill fell from her fingers, unbloodied. By the time Bartholomew had collected and returned it to her, Kulika's uncertainty had crept back in.

She hesitated, and the gong rang again.

'Sir,' said a young Silver Kulika didn't recognise, long-haired and anchor-bearded, like a knock-off Bartholomew Roberts from his pirating days.

'Not now,' Bartholomew said irritably, not breaking eye contact with Kulika.

The knock-off pirate cringed, but persisted. 'The thing is, sir, there are a lot of them tonight, and if we're going to get through them all before—'

'This can wait,' Kulika said decisively, laying the quill back across the pages of the book. She needed time to think, and the ceremony would give her that.

The gong rang again.

It was tolling midnight, Kulika belatedly realised.

With one last, frustrated glance at Kulika, Bartholomew closed the book with a snap, sealing the quill inside. He turned to the knock-off pirate. 'Go, then,' Bartholomew said brusquely. 'Get back downstairs.'

Then he pulled up his hood, offered Kulika his arm, and escorted her down the staircase into the candlelit darkness below, trapping her hand against his body where it looped around his arm.

Kulika had a horrible suspicion that now he'd got this far, he wasn't going to let her go until her blood was on the page.

21

IT WAS LATE when the crowd assembled in the largest common area of the block. Quick remembered thinking it was a huge, sprawling space when she'd first seen the room during Monty's brief tour, but now they were packed in here like sardines between the sofas, side tables, bean bags and chairs that littered the room, it felt tiny.

Judging by a quick count of the shining eyes amongst those immediately surrounding her, about half of the crowd were vampires, and most of those were women. Most of the humans were men. It was easier to get the boys here, Xiaoyu had told her down in the cellar. All the vampires had to do was stick a pretty picture on a dating app, say they were up for anything and give the address, then the young idiots came rushing incautiously to their doom. Most women were more circumspect, more suspicious. It took trust to get them to the mansion, which meant a time investment from the vampire looking to lure them.

Not from Monty, though. All he'd had to do was bat his pretty long eyelashes and bait her with the promise of finding one of her missing people, and Quick had come running.

Like an idiot.

Looking at Monty now, standing beside her with a proprietorial gleam in his eye, she was struggling to think of anyone she loved less.

She'd tried. She'd kissed him up on the roof, danced with him in the dorms, and even attempted a bit of a fumble, but it had been clumsy and wrong and it made her feel like dirt. Quick was fast realising that she just didn't like Monty that much. In fact, after everything that he'd done, she thought she might hate him. Evita used to say that love and hate weren't all that far away from each other, that the true opposite of love was apathy, but now Quick knew that was bollocks. She'd gone from being indifferent about Monty, to being mildly attracted to him, then straight to utter contempt for him as a person and a vampire. That was a one-way track that she didn't see any hope of reversing back down, not while there was so much more contempt already rushing down the line behind her, pushing her along.

It didn't matter that her life was at stake, and any hope of finding Evita with it. It didn't matter that Monty was the only vampire in this room who even knew her name. She was starting to think that anyone else might be a better choice for the Casting.

'Right, listen up,' said Brandon, the long-haired pirate-looking guy from the night of the pool party, the bastard who'd conspired with Monty to start this nightmare. He was standing on a table, raising his voice to get the attention of the room, who were mostly ignoring him.

Until Bella hopped up beside him.

'Shut the fuck up!' she yelled. 'Listen carefully or you fucking die!' She glared around the room, daring anyone to so much as whisper, then hopped back down to the ground when she was satisfied that they wouldn't, ceding the table to Brandon again.

'Crazy,' Monty whispered to Quick, making an unkind gesture as he did so. 'Like I said.'

'Right,' Brandon said from his perch. 'There's a lot of us tonight, so here's how it's going to go. We're going in one line, single file, from here through the wardrobe – humans first and Silver behind, except I'll lead us out. When you get to the wardrobe, you find a cloak that fits and put it on with the hood up, then follow me over to the house. When we get there, you pick up a candle from the stack by the door and light it from the candle of the person in front of you. When we're in the hall, the Silver line up against the wall by the door, humans by the wall on the other side of the room. Questions?'

There were none, or at least none that anyone was brave enough to ask.

'Good,' said Brandon. 'When you're all lined up, Bartholomew's going to call you forward one by one. When he says your name, you move to the foot of the stairs and take your hood away from your face. He'll ask you who's going to try and turn you, you point out the Silver you want, and that's your bit done. Questions? No? Off we go, then.'

Monty pushed her towards the door, and there was no time to think after that.

The wardrobe was a scrum, with people grabbing and snatching and all the time the rest of the queue pushing them from behind. Quick ended up with a robe that she was sure was intended for a man, if the width of the shoulders was any measure. Despite her height, the hem trailed on the floor to be trodden on – frequently – by the person behind her. At least the walk to the house was mercifully short.

It was lonely, walking hooded and single file, strongly suspecting she was the only human in the line who didn't want this. She felt isolated in the darkness. She thought about running, just legging it across the grass to the river. Then she remembered the man from that morning, and the alligators. Which probable death would she prefer, one by Monty's teeth, or at the teeth of an alligator?

It's just a bite, he'd told her earlier that evening. *You drink a taste of my blood, then I drink yours, and it's done. It'll be over in no time. You'll see.*

Or, she supposed, she wouldn't. She was almost certain, in fact, that after Monty bit her she wouldn't be seeing much of anything at all, not with any kind of sanity. If she let Monty bite her, she'd be waking up as a zombie. In those circumstances, maybe she'd be better off trying her luck with the gators. She might have done exactly that, but they were already at the house now, and there were vampires everywhere.

She'd missed her chance.

There were more robe-clad humans waiting for them by the pool, about the same number again as those coming from the block. When Brandon had said there were a lot of them tonight, he wasn't kidding. Quick couldn't imagine how they were all going to fit into one room.

That became clear the moment they stepped inside, through the main door at the front of the house. The hallway was enormous, more a ballroom than an entrance hall, lit only by candles placed here and there on the walls and in standing candelabra. The ceiling stretched up three floors above their heads. To the left, a grand staircase swept up to the first floor, where a mezzanine ran around every side of the room, wider on the wall opposite the staircase than it was along either side. From the banisters at that wide edge, a dimly-lit cluster of figures dressed in dark robes looked down on the gathering.

'Candle,' someone said, snapping Quick's attention back down to ground level. She'd been staring up, she realised, and she'd forgotten what she was supposed to be doing. It seemed like ages now since she'd last slept, and she was starting to panic, so concentration was in short supply.

The woman in front of her was holding out her lit candle, gesturing Quick to the pile of unlit tapers on the table to her side. Quick grabbed one and, after a bit of confusion, managed to light it off the one the woman was offering. That done, Quick made to follow her across the hall to the far wall where a crowd of hooded, candlelit figures was already arrayed, only to be jerked back by her robe. At first, she thought the person behind her had stood on the hem again, then he said, 'You have to give me a light!' and she realised her error.

By the time that was all sorted out, Quick was flustered and shaky and sweating under her robe. The crowd of humans waiting opposite parted in front of her as though they were worried they might catch her lack of poise, which was fine by Quick. It gave her a clear path to the wall, where she could lean and think and try to come up with a way out of this mess.

She could only hope that her name was called somewhere close to last.

22

FROM THE BALCONY on the first floor mezzanine, Kulika had a clear view of the floor below. Bartholomew had insisted that she stay there, by his side, hooded at his right hand like a dark bride. *This is what I'm offering you*, the gesture said. *All my power, all these Silver under your control, and more to come.*

Kulika couldn't deny that it was impressive in its scope, if repugnant in its conceit. She'd never seen a Casting ceremony with so many candidates. It was going to take all bloody night. The humans were moving one by one to the centre of the hall beneath them as Bartholomew called their names from a list he pulled from the back of his covenant book. Once the human had called out the name of the Silver they'd chosen to attempt their turning – a novelty, since usually the Silver did the choosing – the matched pair moved to a side room and didn't return.

Kulika didn't want to imagine what was going on in that side room any more than she wanted to remember what she'd nearly agreed to upstairs, but the long ceremony gave her plenty of time to reflect on both.

She'd nearly signed her life away, and she wasn't at all

certain that she wouldn't actually go through with it before the night was over. Right now, she couldn't come up with a better plan.

'Patience Quick,' Bartholomew intoned beside her.

Kulika's spiralling thoughts slowed abruptly, as though they'd been caught in treacle.

Quick.

Kulika twitched, barely suppressing the impulse to step up to the railing for a better look. But she didn't have to get any closer to recognise Quick once she'd pulled the hood away from her sunset hair, shaking it free so it glimmered in the candlelight.

Kulika felt sick. She could feel eyes on her too, and turned to Bartholomew to see him looking at her with an interest he didn't try to hide. He'd seen her twitch, and he'd probably sensed more besides: the racing of her heart, the tensing of her muscles, and a thousand other tiny signs that her attention was hooked on the woman who stood in the centre of the floor beneath them, waiting for the question Bartholomew was about to ask.

'Whom do you select to turn you Silver?'

Down below, Quick looked like she was scrambling. Her gaze was searching the crowd of young Silver opposite her, looking for something she couldn't find. Even from across the space that separated them, Kulika could feel the nervous energy rolling off Quick in waves, infecting her with the same anxiety.

She should have realised Quick was going to be a candidate tonight; why else would Bartholomew have dragged her out of the buffet line this morning? And now it was too late for Kulika to do anything about it. Quick was going to get bitten, and if what Kulika had heard from Bayly about the mansion's success ratios was true, she was probably going to die. No wonder she was nervous.

Kulika hadn't had a chance to be nervous about her own turning, because she hadn't seen it coming. There had been no Casting ceremony, no ritual, just a visit to the captain's cabin that ended with his blood in her mouth and his teeth in her throat. Perhaps that had been a mercy. Quick would have none of that, but Kulika prayed at least that the bite she received would be less brutal for it.

The hall was quiet as Quick delayed her choice. None of the other candidates had been like this. They'd all walked through the door with a name already on their lips, ready to declare themselves. Quick was different, though. Unlike the others, she didn't seem excited to be here. Her gaze was darting around like that of a startled deer, trying to latch onto something, and failing.

Finally, she looked up at Bartholomew with despair in her eyes, and stilled. Then she pointed at the balcony and said, 'I want her to do it.'

It took a second for Kulika to realise that Quick was pointing at her. During that second, all hell broke loose.

23

QUICK WAS PANICKING. There was no other word for it. She gripped her candle in sweating, shaking hands, worrying at the wax that spilled down over her fingers. She'd known this was coming, known she'd have to choose someone, known that anyone would be better than Monty, but *who*? She didn't know any of these other vamps. She hadn't even exchanged a word with almost all of them. The only names she could remember were Brandon's, who was a bastard – besides which, he'd already been chosen and left the hall – and Bella's, but she seemed like an even worse option than Monty.

She could just point, she supposed. Randomly, into the crowd of vampires, and see where her finger landed.

But was no connection at all *really* better than the unwanted connection she had to Monty? She didn't know, she couldn't work it out, and she was running out of time to decide.

Everyone was waiting.

She had to say a name.

Any name.

Just as Quick had opened her mouth to say 'Monty', her

gaze flicked hopelessly up to Bartholomew, but it landed on the briefly-candlelit face of the woman next to him. The woman Quick had once considered to be her only hope of salvation in this place.

Maybe she'd been right: maybe Kulika would be the one to save her, just not in the way she'd hoped.

So she pointed at her.

It was impulsive, but really, what did she have to lose?

Across the hall, Monty was now the one looking panicked. By contrast, a strange calm was settling over Quick.

'You can't choose from the balcony,' he stage-whispered to her. 'You have to choose from us.'

'Why?' Quick asked.

Monty spluttered for a moment, before saying, 'Because,' which seemed like a stupid reason to her. If she was most likely going to die tonight, then Quick was going to play the cards she'd been dealt the best way she knew how, and she knew in her bones that Kulika was her best way out of here alive. She'd known it from the way her stomach had flipped the moment she'd caught sight of her candlelit face.

If only Kulika was willing to try.

Up on the balcony, what Quick could see of Bartholomew's face didn't look pleased. Kulika was looking at him with open confusion, her hood pulled away from her face now, as the ritual required. Then her eyes found Quick's, and Quick felt the spark.

There was something there.

Wasn't there?

Maybe it was just her desperation talking. Maybe she was kidding herself, but if Kulika would only try…

Bartholomew said something to Kulika, then turned and walked from the balcony. After one more glance at Quick,

Kulika followed him. From the floor above, a door slammed. And they waited.

24

IN THE UPSTAIRS parlour, Bartholomew threw his book onto a spindly little side table with such force that it rocked, then he put his hands on his hips and stared out of the window into the dark night.

'Do you know her?' he asked.

'Barely,' said Kulika, as surprised by what had just happened as he seemed to be. 'I met her for the first time this morning. You were there.'

'And there's nothing between you?' he pressed.

'Nothing,' Kulika replied, but her mind wandered unbidden to sunset hair, grass-green eyes, and the scent of the frosted earth in winter, releasing a knot in her chest that she hadn't known was there.

Kulika felt Bartholomew's attention sharpening on her. He turned to face her.

'You could do it,' he said, clearly sensing more than Kulika had wanted to reveal. 'Couldn't you?'

'No way,' Kulika said. 'I'm not doing to her what you did to me.'

'Because that was the worst thing that ever happened to you.'

181

'It's up there,' she said acidly.

'I gave you immortality.'

'You *cursed* me with immortality,' Kulika yelled. 'I didn't ask for it. All I wanted was freedom, a life where I could travel and be something other than a wife to a tyrant.'

'And that's exactly what I gave you!'

They were shouting at each other now, voices raised and fists clenched.

'No, you just made me first mate to a tyrant instead!'

'You're the one who chose to disguise yourself and run off to a life of piracy,' he argued. 'Without the power I gave you by turning you Silver, you would have been a wife to the whole crew! I didn't want to subject you to that.'

'But you'll subject me to this?' she asked, pointing towards the hall. 'You'll make me bite that girl, risk her life, and—'

'You like her,' Bartholomew said quietly.

'Enough that I don't want to kill her. You know that's exactly what will happen if I try to turn her.'

'I don't think so,' he said, watching her carefully.

Kulika watched him right back.

'Do this for me,' Bartholomew said, 'and I'll give you what you want.'

Kulika stilled. She must have misheard, or misunderstood, because what he'd just offered her made no sense.

'Let me get this clear,' she said slowly. 'If I try to turn Quick Silver, then you'll give me the information you have on Evita Khalyed.'

'Yes,' he said, gritting the word out like the concession pained him, though he made it nonetheless.

'Even if the turning isn't successful?'

'Yes.'

'I won't have to sign anything?'

'You won't have to sign anything,' he said reluctantly. 'I'll let you leave tonight, and all you have to do is attempt to turn one human Silver.'

'And you'll confirm that in writing?' Kulika said.

Bartholomew hesitated for the briefest second before saying, 'In writing.'

'In your own blood.'

He tutted impatiently. 'In whoever's blood you wish.'

It didn't make any sense at all.

'What's your stake in this?' she asked.

'I want to make more Silver. As many as possible. You know that by now.' His words were light, but the look in his eyes was intense.

'But why do you care so much about turning *her*, in particular?'

'Does it matter? You'll get what you want, and I'll get what I want.'

It wasn't explanation enough. Quick *meant* something to Bartholomew, that much was clear. If she didn't, then why would he be willing to give up his strongest bargaining chip – Evita Khalyed's location – when he'd had Kulika on the verge of signing his Articles just hours before?

But, as he'd said, did it matter? Kulika had come here to do one thing: find Evita Khalyed. She couldn't do anything about the fact that Quick's life was on the line, and the woman had made her choice. Quick wanted Kulika to attempt the turning, Bartholomew wanted Kulika to attempt the turning, and if Kulika wanted to save Baron Drake's life – which she absolutely did – then she *needed* to attempt the turning.

So why was she hesitating?

Perhaps her pride was pricked, she thought. Perhaps it hurt that Bartholomew's gaze, so intently focused on her earlier that night, had switched so easily to a new target.

But the more she prodded at Bartholomew, the more likely he was to recant his offer. She couldn't give him time to reconsider, not over something so trivial. Her pride wasn't worth Baron Drake's life.

'All right,' she said, picking up the book and throwing it at Bartholomew. 'Then write it down. A new section, in the back. *Kulika's* covenant.'

25

NO ONE WAS moving in the hall below. Quick heard shouting from upstairs. She couldn't make out the words, but the vampires opposite her were exchanging looks that suggested they could. When they weren't glaring at Quick, that was.

Then a door on the mezzanine above slammed open and Bartholomew returned to his perch. Kulika didn't follow him.

'Patience Quick: return to the line,' Bartholomew said.

Confused, and more than a little scared, Quick did as she was told. None of the other humans had been sent back to the wall, but then none of them had chosen a vampire who wasn't in the diminishing crowd opposite them.

'Phoebe Perrin,' Bartholomew said.

A girl stepped forwards, taking down her hood, then gave the name of her chosen vampire, and the ceremony continued as though nothing had happened. It was as though Quick had never been called on at all, as though Bartholomew had pressed a reset button and erased the previous five minutes.

Did that mean Kulika had rejected her? That Quick would

end up back in the blood bank with the others, feeding the vampires day after day until they bled her dry? Or would she get the chance to make a different choice when the others had made their selections?

No one said anything about it, or even acknowledged what had happened, so she guessed she'd just have to wait and see.

For the next hour, Bartholomew called name after name until the hall was practically empty. At the end, there were just three other humans left in the line with Quick, and ten vampires opposite, including Monty. He was still glaring at her, relentlessly.

When the next girl stepped forward, she glanced nervously back at Quick for a moment before saying, 'Monty.'

He looked at the girl. He looked at Quick. Then he crossed the floor, wrapped his arm around the girl's waist and left without a backwards glance.

That option was off the table, then.

The last two made their choices, one after another, and then it was just Quick on her side, still unhooded, with seven hooded vampires she didn't know facing her across the hall.

Quick looked up at Bartholomew, waiting for him to call her name, but instead there was a rush of air and all the candles went out – including the one Quick was holding – plunging the hall into darkness.

Quick stepped slowly backwards until she could feel the wall behind her shoulder blades, waiting for her eyes to acclimatise to the dark.

She waited.

And waited.

Still, all she could see was black.

There was movement on the other side of the hall. She

heard the door to the outside world opening, caught a brief glimpse of a handful of figures silhouetted against the starlit doorway, then the door closed again and the darkness returned. But at least she knew where the door was now, so she had something to aim for.

Carefully, holding her arms out in front of her, she pushed away from the wall and struck out across the hall, bare feet scuffing along the floorboards. It shouldn't be too much further, she thought. Maybe forty paces in total, so half as much again as she'd already travelled, but every step felt like a mile in the dark.

Then her outstretched hands hit something warm.

She stopped.

The other person snatched.

26

IN THE ROOM upstairs, Kulika was pacing.

The ceremony was interminable. So many candidates. So many Silver. And, she imagined, so much blood in the room beneath her where the turnings were taking place.

She'd watched from the window for a while, counting the bodies coming out through the mansion's back door. With some of them, the ones who were being carried unconscious back to the block, they wouldn't be able to tell for hours whether the transformation had been successful or not. With others, it was clear already. A few of the former humans walked themselves happily back across the lawn with their partners, as newly-transformed Silver. A lot more were dragged, biting and growling, off to the river to feed the alligators.

It was efficient, Kulika had to give him that. Bartholomew had never been one for wasted effort, which was exactly why this situation with Quick was such a puzzle. Kulika had the contract, signed in Bartholomew's blood. She just had no idea why he'd given it up in return for so little from her.

When the door to the room finally slammed open, revealing Quick struggling vainly in Bartholomew's arms,

Kulika was still no closer to an answer.

'Put her down,' Kulika said.

'She's all yours,' Bartholomew replied, plonking Quick into the nearest armchair. She looked flustered, pink-cheeked and wild-haired. It affected Kulika more than she liked to admit.

Bartholomew closed the door, but he was still on the inside of it.

'Leave us,' Kulika said.

'That wasn't part of the deal,' he replied.

'I thought you wanted this to work?'

Kulika stared him down, hands on her hips, feet planted firmly, braced for a fight. For a moment, she thought she might get one, but eventually he reached for the door again.

'I'll be right outside,' he said, then he left.

Kulika knew he hadn't gone far. She could hear him out on the mezzanine, listening and waiting, which meant she would have to be careful how she played this.

'What's happening?' Quick asked her, combing her unruly hair back from her face.

Kulika wished she could help, but she held herself back.

'He wants me to give you what you asked for,' she said instead.

'But you...' Quick looked away for a moment, then looked back at Kulika nervously and said, 'But you don't want to?'

'Irrelevant,' she lied. 'He made me an offer I couldn't refuse.'

An offer that was still suspicious enough to have Kulika on high alert, but she'd been in that state for hours now, and it was grating on her. She was tired of fighting, tired of scheming, tired of pouring all her energy into staying one step ahead of Bartholomew. Whatever he wanted from

Quick, he'd got it, and Kulika was about to get what she wanted, too. What she needed now was to stop fighting and get the job done.

Kulika dropped down into the armchair opposite Quick, tracing her features with her gaze. She looked younger tonight, not physically but in the youthful innocence of her wide, shining eyes. She had no idea what she'd landed herself in the middle of, that much was clear.

'Why would you put me in this position?' Kulika asked, almost plaintively. 'You don't know me. We aren't anything to each other.' Kulika blinked as the realisation settled heavily in her stomach: they were nothing to each other, which meant…

'If I try to do this, then I'm going to kill you.'

'I'm sorry,' Quick replied firmly, 'but you're my best chance.'

Kulika shook her head, but there was no way out of this now. Quick was set on this course of action, Kulika had already agreed to it, and the blood was on the page.

'Let's get it over with, then,' Kulika said, getting to her feet.

'First, tell me what it'll be like,' Quick asked, looking up at Kulika with something close to desperation. She needed something to cling to, Kulika realised. An order of things, a process that she could follow so she didn't have to concentrate on the bigger truth looming at the end of the line.

Kulika tried to put the process into words, but the reality of her own turning was distorted by trauma and time. The pieces she remembered were the ones she wished she could forget, the moments of clenched fists and lost dignity and a pain that was so intense that it had felt distant only hours after the event, not to mention centuries. So instead she asked herself: what would she have wanted to know before her turning, if she'd had the choice? But again, she'd suppressed too much of the experience to have any idea what to say.

There was one thing she could offer Quick, though. She'd learned enough since her own transformation to know that you didn't have to turn someone the way she had been turned, with violence.

'It won't hurt,' Kulika promised, taking Quick's hand to pull her to her feet.

Quick looked confused. 'But, the biting,' she said, letting herself be pulled.

'It can be painful, sometimes. It doesn't have to be, if you'll let me…'

'If I'll what?'

But Kulika couldn't bring herself to say the words. Ever since she'd first seen the sunset-haired woman three nights ago, shining across the grotty squalor of Bartholomew's pool party, she'd been drawn to her. She'd wanted to run her fingers through her fiery hair – no, she'd wanted to bury her face in it and inhale. Now that she was beginning to learn the kaleidoscopic scent of English hedgerows, Scottish summers and Spanish orchards that belonged to her, she could barely think straight. She wanted to press her hands into the small of Quick's back and pull her close. She wanted to lean in until her lips were touching Quick's own. She wanted to taste her so badly that her hands hurt with the tension of holding herself back.

Kulika's gaze flickered over Quick's face, pinging like a pinball between the freckles scattered across her cheeks, the generous curve of her lips, the shining hint of dark desire in the dilation of her eyes, until Kulika was dizzy with it.

Then, without Kulika saying a word, Quick reached out a

hand and curved it around Kulika's neck, stroking her fingers behind her ear so they came to rest against Kulika's undercut, rasping through the short hairs. She shivered involuntarily with the pleasure of it and Quick's face froze, then she started to draw her hand away.

'No,' Kulika said, snatching Quick's hand with her own so she could return it to its place. 'Don't stop.'

Then, tentatively, she ran her own fingers into the strands of sunset that had been haunting her for the past three days. They felt like silk, warmed by the heat of Quick's body. Kulika wondered how they would feel pillowed on her shoulder, fisted in her hungry hands, draped across her naked chest.

She looked into Quick's eyes, trying to find a moment of hesitation. If this wasn't what she wanted, if *Kulika* wasn't what she wanted, then she'd drop her hands, step back and break her bargain with Bartholomew. If this wasn't what Quick wanted...

'Yes?' Kulika whispered, leaning in close.

'God, yes,' Quick said.

And Quick kissed her.

27

KISSING KULIKA WAS like… Quick had no idea what it was like. She'd never experienced anything even remotely similar, except for maybe that one time she'd been trying to fish a bagel out of the toaster with a knife and accidentally electrocuted herself. It was overwhelming, and shocking, and she wouldn't have been surprised to find that she'd burned herself in the process.

Then Kulika had started kissing Quick back, her tongue making the briefest contact with Quick's lips, and Quick forgot to breathe. Kulika tasted of the sea, clean and fresh and beckoning her beneath the waves.

She wanted her.

Kulika actually *wanted* her. Quick could feel it in the pressure of her lips, and in the way she'd grabbed for Quick's hand, then run her fingers through her hair… There was no way to misread that.

Was there?

Unless what Kulika really wanted was Quick's blood. She was a vampire, after all.

Oh.

Quick knew she had a long-practised habit of assuming

193

she was unwelcome, but in her defence her assumptions had often proved true. First there'd been her stepfather, who'd alienated her from her mother during the last years of her illness; then her aunt and uncle, who'd changed their minds about formally adopting her the moment she got into a fight at school; then the entire foster system, which passed her around one negligent home after another, each of them interested only in the cheques they got for keeping her. In fact, ever since she'd been four years old, no one in the world had seemed genuinely pleased to have her in their lives, not until Evita. It felt naïve to imagine she might ever find another person who cared.

But maybe that didn't matter. If Quick was a vampire, she'd be strong. She'd be fast. She'd be immortal. With all that power, maybe she could finally find Evita, or at least find out what had happened to her.

'Are you ready?' Kulika asked.

Even if Kulika only wanted Quick for her blood, maybe that was okay, if she was only willing to make Quick strong, like her.

Quick looked into Kulika's grey eyes and said, 'Yes.'

While Quick watched, keeping eye contact all the time, Kulika very deliberately bit her own lip, until beads of blood formed around her teeth.

'Still ready?' she asked through bloody lips.

'Yes,' Quick said, and if her reply was more tentative this time, it didn't stop Kulika from lowering her lips back to Quick's, filling her mouth with copper and her mind with confusion. This felt… wrong, yes, but better than it should. Quick found herself licking her lips when Kulika pulled away, which puzzled her, but then Kulika's mouth was at her neck, kissing a trail across her throat, and Quick stopped caring if any of it was wrong, or strange. She wanted to feel it, and feel it all, the kisses and licks and nibbles all culminating in the tantalising scratch of Kulika's teeth as they grazed her skin and—

When Kulika bit, the world exploded into fireworks of pleasure, and Quick exploded with it.

28

SOMETHING HAD GONE wrong. Something had gone terribly, horribly, awfully wrong, and Kulika didn't understand how.

She'd needed to kiss Quick, not just because she'd wanted to, but because that was how the process worked. The Silver kissed the human, which produced a scent mark that clung to that human and shielded them from the pain of the bite. Kulika didn't understand the science behind it, but she knew that it worked in practical terms, so that's what she'd done.

What she hadn't expected was her reaction to smelling her scent mark mingled with the seasonal delights of Quick's personal perfume. If Kulika had thought that turning Quick Silver would change the alluring variability of her scent, she'd been wrong: it had done nothing but intensify it. It was overwhelming, and despite her intention to be careful, Kulika had lost control entirely. She kissed, she grabbed, she bit. It spun her around and muddled her mind, the mixed aroma of land and sea, as though between the two of them they could contain the whole world. The thought was grandiose and ridiculous, but it settled in her chest like an incontrovertible truth.

When she felt the tingling in her eyes as she tasted Quick's blood, it was barely a surprise. She'd spent the past few days following Quick's flame-red hair like a beacon through the labyrinth of this dark mansion, so was it really any wonder that Quick had turned out to be the object of all her desires?

In short: Kulika had silvered.

She didn't know what it was supposed to feel like, and stories of the sensation were few and far between, but she didn't need to look in a mirror to know that the silver in the whites of her eyes was now suffusing the grey of her irises. She *knew* it, the same way she knew up from down, and she knew where her hands were when her eyes were closed. Kulika had found the missing part of herself, and it was in her arms. *She* was in her arms.

Kulika released her bite and drew back to find Quick looking up at her with silver in the whites of her eyes. God, she was beautiful. With their new silver surroundings, her irises twinkled like emeralds set in white gold, gleaming in the candlelight.

'Did it work?' Quick asked.

'It worked,' Kulika replied.

More than worked, she thought. Though she needed no confirmation of her new feelings, Kulika found that too: in the bite mark at Quick's neck. It wasn't bleeding, because the wound had been sealed with silver, healed by Kulika's new bond to Quick. Her other wounds were gone, too: the bite mark on the other side of her neck, and the bite on her arm.

'You got lucky,' Kulika said. *We both got lucky*, she thought. If Quick hadn't survived the transformation, then the bond would have dragged Kulika to the grave along with her.

'I want you to know that this isn't why I came here,' Quick said, a little bashfully. 'I didn't even know— I came here looking for a friend who went missing last year.'

'I came here looking for someone too. Then I found you.' Kulika smiled, tucking a strand of hair behind Quick's ear, then whispered impulsively, 'Do you want to get out of here?'

She didn't want Quick in this place, with its demons and its ghosts and its bad memories, not to mention Bartholomew lurking outside every door. She could find another way to track down the information she needed for the baron, but right now her priority was getting Quick as far away from the mansion as possible, beyond Bartholomew's reach, before he convinced either of them to sign his covenant.

They could go out of the window. Kulika could carry Quick if she needed to, and fight her way past anyone who tried to stand in her way. If they could make it as far as the river, they could steal a boat and get to Charleston proper, then there were planes and ships across the ocean and, hell, she'd *swim* it if that would get Quick safely back to Britain and away from him.

He would have heard their discussion. By now, he would know that the transformation had worked. And that meant they had to leave now.

Right now.

29

BEING BITTEN BY Kulika was nothing like being bitten by Monty. For starters, Monty had savaged her neck like a wild animal, while Kulika sunk her teeth into Quick's skin in the same way she kissed: with focus and precision, as though she meant to do it well.

And the kiss.

When Kulika had told her being bitten didn't need to hurt, she had told the entire truth. It hadn't hurt at all. Instead, it had burned through Quick like lightning, setting every nerve alight in the most pleasurable, outrageous way imaginable. For a moment afterwards, she could do nothing but catch her breath. Then, all she could do was watch.

Kulika's eyes were sparkling with silver, gunmetal threaded with platinum. If Quick looked into them for very much longer, she was certain she'd be so thoroughly hypnotised that she'd do anything the woman suggested.

But not this.

'Come on,' Kulika whispered, tugging her towards the window.

Quick had come here to find Evita. That had not gone to plan, admittedly, but she'd picked up some clues along the way. She knew that missing kids ended up here, and she knew how. She knew that more than one of the vampires had recognised the faces on her playing cards, including Evita's. She also knew, if Monty was to be believed, that this all had something to do with someone called Jane – or maybe that Evita had been going by a pseudonym – and that the mere mention of *that* name was enough to make Bella lose her mind entirely.

An hour ago, Quick hadn't been in a position to do anything with that information. Now, things were different. She could feel a new strength suffusing her body, and feel the new sensitivity she possessed. Sounds were louder, lights were brighter, and scents were heightened in a way that seemed to draw her inexorably towards Kulika. She could hear the other woman's slow pulse. She could see the twitching in her muscles as she waited impatiently for Quick to follow her, and part of her wanted to do exactly that. The rest knew that, with this newfound strength, and with the authority that being a vampire would provide her in this place – at least compared with the impotence she'd had as a human – she could surely find the answers she'd come here searching for.

'I can't leave,' Quick said, pulling reluctantly away. 'Not until I find Evita.'

Kulika turned, her gaze sharpening. 'Evita?' she said. 'Please tell me you don't mean Evita Khalyed.'

Hope leapt in Quick's chest. 'You know her?'

'No.' She lowered her voice to a pitch Quick shouldn't have been able to discern, and yet she could. 'Does he know you're looking for her?'

'He who?' Quick asked.

Kulika nodded towards the door.

'Bartholomew? I don't know.' Then Quick finally put her

finger on the change that had been staring her in the face since she'd first opened her eyes after Kulika's bite. 'Your eyes are different,' she said. 'Is it because of what just happened?'

'In a way.'

'What way?'

Kulika threw open the window and said, 'Long story short, it means I'm not leaving this mansion without you. So come on.'

Quick was still trying to work out what that *really* meant when the door opened.

'Leaving so soon?' Bartholomew asked, sauntering inside. He seemed almost friendly to Quick, but then she turned to Kulika and revised her assessment. Kulika's grip on the window ledge was so tight that she was warping the frame, splintering it under her fingers.

That was the first sign of trouble. The ones that followed would be worse.

30

'WE'RE LEAVING,' KULIKA said, striding forward and taking Quick's hand again to pull her out of Bartholomew's reach. If Kulika had any say in the matter, he would never touch her again.

'Oh, I don't think so,' he replied.

'We had a deal,' Kulika pointed out, 'written in your own blood. I did what you wanted, now give me the information you promised me and let us go.'

'You've got it,' he replied nonchalantly, infuriatingly.

'What are you talking about?'

'Dr Khalyed was here,' he conceded. 'Briefly. But I don't have any idea what happened to her after she left, or where she went. The best information I have is sitting in your new girlfriend's pretty little head. She's her best friend, you know. Knows everything about her, inside and out.'

Kulika turned to Quick and looked at her, numbness spreading through her limbs.

'Why are you talking about Evita?' Quick asked, looking between the two of them.

Kulika cracked. All this time she'd been hanging around the mansion, waiting on Bartholomew's pleasure, wasting days on the promise of knowledge he didn't even have. He'd never had anything to give her. He'd bluffed on an empty hand, and she'd gone all in.

'You had nothing. All this time,' she said to him softly, dangerously, then she yelled, 'Nothing!' and kicked out at the nearest side table, splintering it into kindling.

Quick jumped away, putting an armchair between them. Kulika was scaring her, she realised. She should calm down, *discipline* herself, but she couldn't calm down, not now she'd worked out what he'd done. This whole time, he'd been playing her.

Of course he'd been playing her.

'What was the point?' Kulika yelled at Bartholomew. 'I would have signed,' she said, knowing in her heart that it was true: she would have signed his Articles in return for the information she'd thought he held. 'You could have had me, but instead you've just delayed me by days, for no reason at all.'

'You know me better than that,' he replied, leaning casually against the door, pushing it back into its frame until it clicked shut. 'Everything I do is for a reason.'

'Then why even bother? For fun?'

'Please, Kulika. I'm a businessman these days, not a pirate. I work for the rewards that profit me, not merely for my own amusement. But I've fulfilled my part of the bargain. You have your information. Pick Ms Quick's brains as much as you wish, and then you can leave.'

'I'm not staying here another minute,' Kulika said.

'Then you'll leave with nothing,' Bartholomew replied. The first hints of a smile began to tug at the corner of his mouth. 'Because, you see, Ms Quick is staying here with me.'

'No, she's not,' Kulika replied with equal assurance. 'I

turned her, and I'm claiming her. She doesn't belong to you, Bartholomew. She's not wearing your mark. She hasn't signed your covenant.'

'Hasn't she?' Bartholomew asked, his smile becoming ever more evident. Then he pulled a new leather-bound book from his robes, one that Kulika didn't recognise, and opened it to a page covered in red signatures. 'They all sign on their way into the mansion for the Casting,' he said, adding with mock sincerity, 'Oh, dear. Did you not know?'

Kulika looked at Quick as the bottom fell out of her world.

'Outside the main door,' Quick whispered. 'They said we had to. They said—'

'So you see, Kulika,' Bartholomew said, crossing the room to snatch Quick's hand before Kulika could stop him, 'she does, indeed, belong to me.'

He pulled a new object from his robes, a weapon Kulika recognised with a sharp chill of fear.

Kulika yelled, 'No!'

But it was too late. Bartholomew had already uncurled Quick's fingers and slammed the stamp into her palm, while Kulika stood by hopelessly and watched.

Quick screamed.

Kulika's blood froze.

It was a crude thing, that stamp: a vicious cluster of needles fed by a well of ink at their base, designed by Bartholomew himself with utility rather than comfort in mind. Kulika remembered all too clearly how it had felt when he had ground the pointy end into her own skin, leaving behind a dirty black wound that had bound her to his crew for all eternity. At least until Baron Drake had come along.

Kulika rushed to Quick's side, wrapping her arms

protectively around her as Quick cradled her bleeding palm. It would heal soon enough now that she was Silver, but Kulika knew from experience that the stain would remain, Bartholomew's black mark sealed deep under the skin.

Quick was bound to Bartholomew.

Kulika felt sick.

Quick, the woman Kulika had just turned, had just silvered for and, undeniably, had just fallen for, pitching headfirst into a love from which the only possible escape was death.

'That's why you wanted me to turn her,' Kulika whispered to Bartholomew. Even to her own ears, her tone sounded like an admission of defeat. 'You knew I would silver.'

'I guessed,' Bartholomew conceded, sheathing the stamp. 'You were showing… How to say this delicately? Signs of partiality?' He was smiling like a wolf now, no longer bothering to hide his triumph. He opened the book to the page of signatures once more, and pointed at one in the centre that read, *Patience Quick*. Even from this distance, Kulika could scent that it was written in Quick's own blood.

'As it turns out, I didn't need you to sign my covenant,' Bartholomew said to Kulika, tapping the signature with a grin. 'Not when I already have your heart right here.'

He slammed the book shut, and the noise was like a chain wrapping around Kulika's throat.

Then he laughed.

And laughed.

If you enjoyed *Kill Me Quick*, why not read *A Quick Study*? It's the second book in the *QuickSilver* trilogy, and it carries on right where *Kill Me Quick* left off.

***

Join my Readers' Club and receive a FREE short story

www.josiejaffrey.com/subscribe

***

Please leave a review!

If you enjoyed *Kill Me Quick*, I'd be so grateful if you would please review it. Book reviews can make a huge difference to the success of a novel, particularly those of self-published authors like me. If you have time to leave a review, even if it's just a sentence or two, then I'd really appreciate it.

***

Explore the rest of the Silverse…

This book is just one small part of the Silverse, a whole world of vampires that's waiting for you to explore. There are more novels, short stories, serialised story episodes, and even audio drama podcasts. They're all interrelated, although each series stands alone.

Find out more on my website at www.josiejaffrey.com

Acknowledgements

The QuickSilver series has been a decade in the making. It pulls together threads of story littered over hundreds of years' of world-building, and spread across three other separate novel series and a stack of short stories. Finding those threads and lining them up properly to write this central puzzle piece of the Silverse apocalypse has been an absolute undertaking, and one I would never have been able to manage without the unfailing support of my editor Adie Hart. She goes above and beyond to make sure that I haven't borked the continuity or introduced inconsistencies that will tie me in knots later, and she does so with the kind of enthusiasm that keeps me writing when nothing else would. Thank you so much, A, for everything you do.

Huge thanks also to Jen Sugden, my personal cheerleader and bookseller, and wonderful fellow author. I would not have been able to become an audio fiction writer without your support, and I can't wait to explore the podcast world further with you. Big love.

Thanks also to my author buddies Ali Clack and the UKYA Authors Instagram group for their company and support, and to Rachel Bowdler and the Swords & Sapphics Discord for writing with me. Without the sprints channel in that Discord group, I seriously doubt that this series would have been completed so quickly, and I certainly wouldn't have had as much fun doing it.

And thanks to my street team the Silverse Squad, for their unfailing support in promoting my books. I am so grateful.

Finally – and always – thank you to my husband and son, for everything.

CONTENT WARNINGS

General warning for violence/murder.

General warning for graphic blood/gore, including consensual and non-consensual blood drinking, description of injuries, dead bodies.

Sexual content (mostly consensual, some dubiously consensual due to coercive control).

Some swearing (up to and including 'fuck').

Cannibalism and ritual murder/dismemberment.

Cult-like community with coercive control.

Mentions of slavery and killing of enslaved people, both in real/historical context and fantastical/modern context, including keeping humans imprisoned for use as a blood bank.

Discussion of historical piratical crimes.

Emotionally abusive/coercive relationships, including family.

Uncomfortably sexual behaviour from a quasi-father figure.

www.ingramcontent.com/pod-product-compliance
Lightning Source LLC
Chambersburg PA
CBHW010436170726
48283CB00011B/3230